Out of Poland

AWARD-WINNING
Breakfield and Burkey
A Novella

Out of Poland
by Charles V Breakfield and Roxanne E Burkey
© Copyright 2021, ICABOD Press
ALL RIGHTS RESERVED

With certain exceptions, no part of this book may be reproduced in any written, electronic, recording, or photocopying form without written permission of the publisher or author. The exceptions would be in the case of brief quotations embodied in critical articles or reviews and pages where permission is specifically granted in writing by the author or publisher and where authorship/source is acknowledged in the quoted materials.

This book is a work of fiction. All names, characters, places, and incidents are the products of the authors' imaginations or are used fictitiously. Any resemblance to actual events, locales, or people living or dead is coincidental.

Published by

ICABOD Press

ISBN: 978-1-946858-53-5 (Paperback)
ISBN: 978-1-946858-54-2 (eBook)
ISBN: 978-1-946858-44-3 (Audible)

Library of Congress Control Number: 2021911051
First Edition — Novella

Cover, Interior and eBook design by Rebecca Finkel, FPGD.com
Cover map is with the permission of https://omniatlas.com/maps/europe/19390916/

Printed in the USA
HISTORICAL FICTION | SUSPENSE

Author's Foreward

It is 1939 Europe. Germany is on the march for land and wealth across Europe. The future founders of the R-Group are young military men willing to fight for their country and their beliefs. The final direction of fighting for their families, friends, and honor leads to an unexpected decision. This story is the historical beginning of our current generation of the R-Group of the 21st century. Lessons learned here are the foundation of why the R-Group for generations are committed to fighting tyranny in any form.

Prologue

"Honestly, Ferdek, Europe is engulfed in madness. The wives I lunched with yesterday were beside themselves discussing correspondence from friends across Europe, of the boldness of Germans. I fear this is far from over. Are we going to avoid this mess? How much will our lives change, darling?" Gretta sipped her coffee and affectionately smiled at her husband of nearly thirty years.

"My darling wife, you have been my strength for so many years. Our children's compassion comes from your influence." Smiling with affection, Ferdek adds, "Our daughter, Patrycja, has the grace, beauty, and poise much like you possessed when we met. And Ferdek is so full of honor and determination for someone so young. I am proud he joined the military to fight for our country, but I'm glad to have him reassigned closer to home. I love the family we've created, but the madness you mention is approaching.

"We can only go so far with diplomacy. I am trying to negotiate. Getting support from our allies is our biggest challenge. You would think all Europeans would remember the devastation of the great war and avoid this fighting. I know the noise and combat are ripping across the continent. The lunatic Hitler wants the ultimate control, and his ego knows no bounds. You're right; the times seem bleak with this test for humanity.

"Our Poland is a proud country with brave, honorable men who are willing to fight to protect their families and friends. We are, however, not a military-machine like Germany." Ferdek finished his toast and coffee, gently wiping his mouth with the embroidered napkin. Soundlessly moving back his chair by the crafted arms, he stood. Swiftly straightening his jacket and checking his cuffs, he smiled at his bride.

Walking over to Gretta, he patted her slender shoulder and kissed her cheek. "Darling, just to be prepared in advance, please start to assemble some luggage. Pack clothes for each of us, currency, and information on our key contacts outside of Poland."

A flicker of fear crossed her beautiful face before she smiled at the love of her life. "Of course, I'll get some things ready, but I'm certain we won't need it unless we get to enjoy a weekend getaway. One bag each, right?"

Ferdek resolutely smiled and bent to kiss her again. "I promise to let you know of changes when I can. You are my greatest confidant. I know somehow, we will survive. I don't know how yet. I may be at the office a little late. Don't hold supper."

"Ferdek, you have the best interest of Poland at heart. Please be careful." She said as she held his hand for an extra second. "We are stronger together. I trust you. Please believe I am here for you always."

Chapter 1

Ambassador Ferdek Watcowski stands on the balcony of the Royal Castle, Poland's seat of government, looking out across Warsaw. Heavy mist rising from the land coupled with a dark sky make his mood dreary. Somberly, he watches as lights turn off one at a time in buildings scattered across the city.

Watcowski notices a handful of men and women hurrying down the sidewalks with heads bowed against the chill. The wail of an approaching ambulance captures his attention from the people while it passes. A bus, squealing from heavy use and poor maintenance, stops to pick up a lone passenger at the street corner.

Alone with inner thoughts at the scene unfolding outside, his office door clicks open. The air shifts slightly before the door closes. Light footsteps announce his daughter before she gently touches his arm. "Father,

I delivered the correspondence and felt the tension from every person in every department."

Turning toward his beautiful, grown assistant with fondness, he frowns at the shadow of concern marring Patrycja's pretty face and typically bright smile. His eyes drift back out the window of his favorite city. "I fear we are facing the end, my little Patrycja. The Poland you have known for your twenty-two years is no more. I understand their tension as I can almost feel the land we love slipping through our fingers."

"No, Father, the war is only just begun. We are a proud people. We will fight as long as we have breath to fight."

Almost on cue, Ferdek turns toward the distant sound of an explosion, gunfire, and tanks rumbling beyond the peaceful fog. "The German army is nearly at our door, and we have no way to stop them. We have a brave defense force on horseback. The Germans have an army of tanks. We have pitchforks. They have machine guns. We are like lambs before the slaughter. We will indeed fight as long as we have air to breathe. The Germans have us surrounded, with their greedy hands around our throats."

"We must not give up, Father."

Watcowski forces a smile at her determination. "We have hope, Patrycja. We need guns."

"Father, surely there is someone to help us."

"No one, Patrycja. We are alone." Absent-mindedly he wipes the tear escaping from her eye.

"I will pray for the best, Father."

"May God have mercy on us all, little one." He gently embraces her. "I fear the worst is upon us."

Chapter 2

The railroad yard in Gdansk is always a hive of activity with trains coming and going. Men and machines toil to get the rolling cars loaded and unloaded. The overcast sky makes it appear an endlessly gloomy day. Ferdek, the younger, behind a storage barrel studies the comings and goings in the yard. A break in the action occurs. He softly gestures and says, "Come on, fellows." He slowly goes forward, waiting for them. The two men carefully and soundlessly jump from the car where they are hiding. With almost choreographed movements, the three men attempt to blend in with the other railroad workers.

Ferdek, the younger, is the ambassador's son. He, along with Tavius and Wolfgang, are lieutenants in the Polish army. Today they are not in uniforms but instead dressed in ragged clothes, with dark cloth caps pulled low over their eyes. They glance nervously in both directions, then move out among the train cars jammed in the yard.

"Let's move into that group as the shift changes," Wolfgang whispers.

Each man is wearing an old leather backpack like many of the men. They need to use these workers to make their scheduled meeting. A long, mournful whistle from a departing train added to the uncertainty settling on their shoulders.

They hit the shift change perfectly, merging with the outgoing workers. Calm but defiant faces are revealed in the soft light as they try to be inconspicuous. Inner turmoil has them each on high alert, eyes constantly darting from left to right.

Initially, they are making good progress to distance themselves from the train yard until a German troop carrier pulls up and stops in front of the group. Eager troops disgorge to line up in front of a lieutenant standing at attention. A German officer, Major, strides up and quietly states, "We know he's here. We don't know why."

The lieutenant replies, "We will find him, sir. Once we do, what are our orders?"

"Shoot him. We are the masters now," the major states with the hint of a smile.

The lieutenant barks to the troops to stand at attention. These soldiers clutch their rifles and move out, following their squad leader. They trot down the street toward the railroad yard, moving past the cluster of workers surrounding Ferdek, Tavius, and Wolfgang, who instinctively turn their faces away from the squad.

Unexpectedly, the major stops beside the cluster of workers. He grabs an old man and jerks him into the street. He holds out one hand with the other resting on the butt of his Lugar. "Your papers, old man. I'm sure they are in order."

The man nervously rummages through his coat pocket and finally pulls out his papers. His hand trembles as he hands them to the major. After a cursory review of the documents, he hands them back, but the frightened citizen misses, and the papers drop to the ground. He scrambles to retrieve them.

The German major turns to Ferdek, frowns, and snaps his fingers, motioning him to come forward. "Your name?"

Ferdek hesitates. He glances at Tavius then at Wolfgang. Each struggles to keep their anxiety under control while sweating profusely.

The major repeats, "Your name. Now. And your documents. Or you will be shot as a refugee without papers."

Ferdek raises his head in defiance and hoarsely states, "Look around you. Like the others you see, the railroad is my employer. My shift is up, and I'm going home."

Unimpressed, the major presses. "Then you will have papers. I want to see your papers. A man without papers is a man who no longer exists."

Emboldened Ferdek counters, "Poland is a free land, and I am a free man. You're here without an invitation. I do not answer to you."

Unimpressed, the officer slowly removes his 9mm Lugar from its holster and points it as if Ferdek is no more consequential than a fly. "You are sadly mistaken. Poland is no longer free. No one is free of German rule. Your papers or Poland will hold your grave."

Before the drama can go any further, the situation erupts. Suddenly the rail yard workers are battling among themselves, shoved forward, then backward. A young man breaks free and runs wildly down the street.

The major rushes into the street, raises his Lugar, and fires a warning shot into the air. He motions to his lieutenant, who dispatches the soldiers to pursue the fleeing man, with the two officers right behind them.

This drama provides the three men the distraction they need to escape. They hurriedly disappear around the corner, barely glancing over their shoulders. Far behind them, they hear a shot. A moment later, a second shot sounds, followed by angry voices that echo down the street. The three men take off at a dead run down a dark alley toward their meeting destination.

Chapter 3

The low light conditions of the streets after dark instill a bit more confidence in the scruffy-dressed men. Still wary, they constantly scan their immediate area. A few footfalls echo, along with muffled conversations of people hurrying along. After several street crossings and backtracking to avoid contact with roaming German troops, Ferdek pauses at a street corner to look for their target destination. He spots a pub sign called the U Szkota and confirms it is the same as on the torn piece of paper retrieved from his shoe. The telltale scent of cigarette smoke, music, and quiet laughter comes toward them from the doorway.

Tavius and Wolfgang join up with Ferdek. Tavius asks, "Is this the right pub?" Ferdek nods.

Wolfgang frowns as he sees the time from the clock above the pub sign. "We're late; it's already 7:18."

Clenching his jaw muscles, Ferdek admits, "We're here even with everything running against us."

With forced mockery, Tavius adds, "And we don't yet need the graves the Germans offered us. Ha."

Ferdek looks down toward the end of the street. A squad of German soldiers is marching toward them. The precision marching sounds of their hobnail boots on the deserted cobblestone street prompt the three to dart into the pub. The sounds of the soldiers do not permeate the noisy establishment.

The interior of the pub is dark, with lit candles burning atop each of the tables. It is a gathering place for workers in dirty clothing on their way home. A few girls dressed in short, tight-fitting skirts, seductive sweaters, and black stockings wander from table to table. The girls serve drinks but also look for additional work. The place throbs with the low hum of voices and an occasional laugh. The patrons come here searching for hope but only seem to contribute to the oppressive atmosphere, even with the worn-out music from a jukebox in the background.

The tavern itself has seen better days. It has a long, sturdy weathered surface with men holding their drafts and quickly talking. A lone barkeep is drying glasses on a ragged towel. His pace is unrushed, but nothing escapes his attention. Ferdek, Tavius, and Wolfgang find an empty table in the corner and sit down. Ferdek takes the chair facing the door with Tavius and Wolfgang flanking him. A fourth chair sits empty, waiting for its guest.

With most of their anxiety in check, Tavius asks, "Now what? We got here late."

Focused on the pub entrance, Ferdek grimly nods, "We wait."

"Jasiek should be here already," suggests Wolfgang, glancing at the other patrons.

Unwaveringly watching the entrance, Ferdek comments, "We are at war. Nothing is guaranteed. Not even time."

Tavius, nervously surveying the interior. "You think he's coming?"

Ferdek confidently straightens. "If he's alive, he'll be here."

"How can you be so sure?" Wolfgang petitions while comparing the workers, looking for inconsistencies.

Ferdek shifts his gaze from between his friends. "He's my father's uncle. He is family. He is one of us."

Tavius shakes his head in disbelief, then throwing both hands up in defeat. "He's an old man."

Ferdek, smirks. "The pistol he carries is old, too, older than he is. But it has killed more than one German. Have some patience, gentlemen."

A dark-haired girl stops. She is dressed like the other waitresses but still a teenager. She leans closely toward Wolfgang, wearing a practiced smile that only comes from confidence at having mastered her discipline. "I've not seen you here before. I'm called Halina. What can I get for you men?"

Wolfgang's attempt to sound convincing falls short. "We only stopped for this night. We'll be gone by morning."

Emboldened, Halina laughs. "One night is enough. Halina can make sure it's a night you won't soon forget."

Ferdek was annoyed at her fearless attitude. "I am sorry, but you must go and practice your business elsewhere. We are meeting someone."

With a bit of flirty hip and raised eyebrows, Halina presses, "A girl, perhaps?"

Tavius blurts out. "No."

But Ferdek quickly corrects the comment. "Yes, a girl, perhaps."

Halina is pleased that she agitated the men as she walks seductively away, glancing back over her shoulder, smiling at her distraction. "You'll be sorry."

Tavius tersely mutters, "I'm already sorry."

Ferdek, grateful Halina has left, offers a halfhearted smile. "It's our loss, I'm sure."

Tavius stares, frowning directly at Ferdek, and demands, "What's that all about? We're not meeting a girl."

Irked, Ferdek counters, "Do you know this girl who calls herself Halina?"

Tavius drops his gaze and shakes his head. "Never saw her before."

"What do you know about her?" Ferdek continues.

Watching her leave, Wolfgang wistfully offers, "She is terribly young… And desperately pretty."

Not willing to drop the lesson, Ferdek challenges, "Is she Polish? Or is she German? Or is she sleeping with a German, and how much would he pay her to find out who we are and why we are here? One wrong word to the wrong person, and tomorrow will come without us."

Wolfgang thoughtfully studied the situation. "Her name is Polish if that is her real name."

Tavius looks remorseful. "Sorry, Ferdek. I wasn't thinking. We shouldn't be so trusting."

Satisfied that he made his point, Ferdek concludes, "It's quite simple, my friends. The less we say, the more the Germans don't know."

Wolfgang takes one last stand of the contrarian position. "Of course, she may have been an innocent working girl trying to survive the night. But then again, I've always been something of a romantic."

Ferdek shrugs. "This a time of war in a land that no longer belongs to us. Nobody is innocent. Innocence lies beneath the tracks of the German tanks. We must drop our gullible and romantic notions. We can only trust ourselves."

Tavius, trying to lighten up their mood, glibly asks, "Not even a pretty girl?"

Not taking the bait, Ferdek coldly states, "She could take a table knife, cut your throat, and never lose her smile."

Wolfgang snaps, "You don't trust anyone, do you, Ferdek?"

"Trust no one. The shadows have eyes, and they are watching us. Even a friend will sell you out for a loaf of bread if he's hungry. We have a job to do tonight. We may fail. We may never see another morning. But we have one chance to stop the German march. For the moment, no one, not even my father, knows we are here or why we are here. That's the way it must remain."

Chapter 4

The dim glow of a streetlamp amplifies the tired look of Ambassador Watcowski's face as he steps out onto the sidewalk. At 6 p.m., his workday thankfully finished, he looks in both directions before walking briskly toward the heart of Warsaw. He is wearing a heavy overcoat which protects him from the windy bursts of the fall night. His face and heart sadden further with each step he takes.

Plodding toward his destination, small snatches of everyday life cross his path. In hushed tones, a mother grabs the hands of her two children and hurries them down a side street. Their steps echo retreat. An air raid siren wails on the western side of Warsaw.

He almost smiles when two lovers stop their passionate embrace on a doorstep with a light turning on at an adjacent window. They hold hands for a moment, staring at each other in desperation, then break apart. Each rushes away in the opposite direction. Ferdek's speculation on the lovers is abruptly interrupted when two police vehicles race down the street.

Approaching his destination, three Polish uniformed soldiers dart from the bar Mleozny and run toward the sound of the air raid warning. Thinking, the ambassador notes he should be doing the same thing, except his target is the bar. His musings are interrupted when an old lady leans over the balcony railing from an upstairs apartment and yells for her husband.

"Jakub. Jakub. It's time you are home. The Germans are coming. Can't you hear the sirens? Jakub don't leave me alone like this. The Germans are on the edge of town."

Almost on cue, the sidewalk is suddenly thick with people pushing and shoving their way out of the bar, scattering down the street. The ambassador watches them for a moment, then enters the Mleozny.

Once inside, he crosses the floor and sits on a stool, and rests his elbows on the bar. The place is virtually empty. The last man at a table near the back tosses back his drink, sets down the glass, and pitches the waitress a silver coin. He reluctantly heads toward the door.

The Mleozny waitress calls to the departing customer, "It's early."

He hollers over his shoulder, "It's early to die."

"Where are you going?"

He turns slightly. "As far away from here as I can."

Laughing and in a mocking tone, she queries, "And leaving me behind?"

In a bleak tone, he adds, "Before the week is over, you will be serving krupnik to Germans."

Annoyed at the statement, she stomps her feet. Her ruddy face appears disgusted, like she swallowed cod liver oil. "Maybe I will throw krupnik in their faces."

Tired of the exchange, the man shoves his hat onto his head. "I will not be back for the funeral." He disappears out the door.

Stanislaw, the owner of Mleozny, pours straight krupnik in a glass for Ferdek. The ambassador eyes the golden liquid then moves his gaze to the bartender.

Stanislaw offers the drink silently with his eyes. "I have not seen you in a long time, Ferdek. I remember the days when you were in here at least once a week for a dance and a kiss and a glass of krupnik."

Lifting the glass to eye level, the ambassador sadly laments, "Those were good days, Stanislaw."

Nodding, Stanislaw replies, "I miss them."

"So do I, Stanislaw. But life takes strange turns. And I fear that we are at a crossroad. We are doomed no matter which way we go."

"The Germans are at our door and will take our liberty," Stanislaw offers.

"And the Russians are at the other one ready to take our soul. It's hard to decide who is the most ruthless."

Stanislaw chuckles softly.

"No, I haven't forgotten our promises for independence. The thoughts we put into words long ago are on my mind when I awaken every morning, Stanislaw. And there they remain all day and long after my day has ended."

Ferdek looks hard at Stanislaw before asking, "What do the people say? You hear them much more clearly than I do. They lie to me because they believe I want them to lie. They tell me we are fighting a war we can win. I don't believe them, Stanislaw. You hear the truth much more clearly than I do. What do you hear?"

"They are afraid, Ferdek. They smell the scent of gunpowder; they feel the tremor of bombs on the edge of Warsaw and are fearful that the land they love will soon drown with their blood."

"Will they fight, Stanislaw, or is it too late?"

"They are a brave people, Ferdek. But they cannot fight tanks with horses, or guns with swords. They won't be marching off to fight, my old friend. They will be marching off to die."

Ferdek holds his glass of krupnik up to the light. He stares at the reflection of the lamp on the liqueur.

He weighs his thoughts for several heartbeats. "I long for the days when my only worries were a dance, a kiss, and a glass of krupnik. Somehow, it all tastes bitter now."

Stanislaw asks, "What will Poland do? What can I tell them?"

The ambassador turns on the stool and stares through an open door into the night. "What indeed."

Chapter 5

Agata wraps her dark wool coat tightly around her to minimize the chill that comes with her movement down the windy sidewalk. Maintaining eyes on her surroundings, she darts between the shadows of the dimly lit storefronts. In her early twenties, she deliberately avoids others like a seasoned spy. Agata is a tall and slender beauty hiding behind her dark hair.

A group of German soldiers, obviously drunk, stagger towards her with their rifles carelessly thrown across their shoulders. Sporadic laughter erupts from the group, and she recognizes the potential trouble with a confrontation. Agata turns abruptly and quickly weaves her way through the traffic to the other side of the street. Her move costs her freedom.

A Gestapo agent appears like a shadow inside the darkness and grabs her arm the moment she steps onto the sidewalk. Stunned for a heartbeat, Agata tries to pull away but can't. She is forced to look at his face a few centimeters away and smells his tobacco breath.

The Gestapo agent growls harshly, "Your name?"

"Agata."

"Occupation?"

"Student."

Now leering and pulling her tightly up against him, he demands, "What are you studying?"

Without warning, Agata kisses him long and passionately. She pulls away, smiling, and replies, "Anatomy." Agata grabs the lapels of his coat, kisses him again, and pushes him toward a nearby opening off the street.

The Gestapo agent follows her lead, and they disappear into the darkness.

A small crowd of people hurries down the sidewalk, unaware of the implicit promises unfolding in the shadows. No one pays heed to the inarticulate noises of first a gasp followed by grunts coming from the alley. Mere moments later, Agata emerges from the passage, calmly wipes the blood off a knife with the agent's handkerchief, then casually tosses the cloth back into the darkness. She slips the knife into her belt beneath her coat. Walking away, she allows the crowd to wrap itself around her, onward to her destination again.

Ferdek, still seated facing the door at the U Szkota Pub, keeps a mental inventory of the people, the activity, and his friends who are nursing their beers. Checking his watch, he knows time is ticking away and still no contact.

After another sip of his beer to remain calm, there's action at the door. The beautiful Agata enters. She stops and looks around. She spots the table and walks straight toward them. Ferdek stands. Agata takes a chair across from him. Her expression is all business. Ferdek sits and studies her in silence. Tavius and Wolfgang sit up straight but seem confused by her calm demeanor. They look at each other and then to Ferdek but say nothing.

In a low but deliberate tone, Agata coolly announces, "I am looking for Ferdek Watcowski."

Starring back at her boldness, Ferdek asks, "And who are you?"

"My name is Agata, but that is not important. I came to the U Szkota to look for a table with three young men. One of them is Ferdek Watcowski. If none of you is known by that name, then I will leave." Receiving no reply, Agata starts to stand and leave.

"I am Ferdek. Why are you looking for me?"

Agata slightly raises her eyebrow in disbelief. "I have a message to give if you are Ferdek."

Tavius hastily asks, "What about?"

Agata ponders a moment. "A certain lock has a certain code that makes Baby operational. I have the code."

Wolfgang eyes her with suspicion mounting and leaning toward the woman far taller even while sitting. "We are to meet a Jasiek, not an Agata."

Pained, she looks away to collect her thoughts. "Jasiek will not be coming tonight."

Ferdek snorts and defiantly adds, "My father trusts only Jasiek when it comes to matters such as this."

After a heavy, ragged breath, Agata offers, "You and your father must learn to trust me."

Ferdek shifts, deliberately placing his big hands on the tabletop. "Why should we? How can we?"

Regaining control of her anguish, Agata says, "Jasiek was an old man. He did what he could for as long as he could, but they killed him."

"Who?"

Studying their faces individually and without emotion, she offers, "You know as well as I do who killed him. Who wants to kill us all and fertilize the land with our blood?"

"I'm sorry. When did it happen?

"Just before sundown. Jasiek suspected what was coming and told me to deliver his message to you."

Leaning forward across the table, Ferdek asks, "Did they learn what information he carried?"

Agata fighting her grief; she shed no tears. "He would not tell them. They cut off his fingers. They dug out his eyes. He would not tell them. I do this for him."

Ferdek presses, "But he told you."

Agata only nodded yes.

Wolfgang and Tavius observe the patrons ensuring no one leaned too close to overhear the discussion between Ferdek and Agata. From experience, they knew Ferdek wouldn't believe a woman because of her beauty.

"Why you? Why tell you?"

Agata passes Ferdek a folded piece of paper and holds it for a second when his fingers reach across. "He was my father."

Ferdeks frowns with empathy. His eyebrows arch as he examines the paper. "The code?"

"Baby is being kept in an abandoned armory on the southern edge of town near the river. On the back is a map that takes you to the vault. There is a key hidden behind the picture of a naked woman." After a moment, Agata continues, "Memorize everything, the code, the map, and then burn the paper."

Ferdek feels more confident in the information. "Have you seen the armory?"

"I have. Not much of a place but all so important."

"How many guards?"

"A squad of sentries outside. Three guards inside the vault room. But that was yesterday. Today brings a new night. What was never is. What is will never be the same again."

Tavius playing devil's advocate, challenges, "What if you're leading us into a trap?

Tired of the cross-examination, Agata stands and pushes the chair away from the table. "That's the chance you'll have to take. Jasiek took the chance. Now it's your turn." She marches across the pub and out the door without a backward glance.

The men sit in silence. Ferdek reads the paper, then holds it up to the candle on the table and lets it burn.

Thoroughly alarmed, Wolfgang admonishes, "Why did you do that? Now you are the only one who knows the code."

A resolved Ferdek nods. "I am."

An exasperated Tavius runs his hands roughly through his unruly hair. "Then what's the plan if something happens to you?"

"The same as it's always been."

Wolfgang presses, "And what exactly is that?"

"Make sure nothing happens to me."

Tavius tries to rationalize the encounter. "What if the girl isn't who she says she is?"

Wolfgang adds, "What if she is working with the Germans?"

Ferdek shrugs. "Only one way to find out."

Both men defiantly stare at Ferdek, who replies, "We open the vault at midnight. If we're still alive at two minutes after midnight, then Agata was telling the truth. Besides that, if she works for the Germans, why lure us into a trap when they could have seized us right here when she asked for Ferdek. I'm betting she is who she says she is."

Wolfgang seems to accept the response though his face reflects his concern. "It's a terrible risk to take in any event."

With eyebrows raised and nodding, Ferdek admits, "It always has been. But we have no other choice."

Smiling sadly, Tavius adds, "Only one thing's for sure. If we die, we no longer have to worry about it.

Chapter 6

The following evening after normal calling hours, Ambassador Watcowski goes to the U.S. consulate in Warsaw. He checks his surroundings then knocks on the door. After a short time, lights come on in the hallway, and U.S. Ambassador Anthony Biddle opens the door, yawning. Biddle shakes Watcowski's hand as he steps outside and looks around, unsure why the Polish ambassador would visit.

Assessing the situation, Biddle queries, "This is certainly unexpected, Mr. Ambassador. I would have never thought you'd be out alone and here at such an ungodly hour, without an escort."

Watcowski nods and comments formally. "I apologize for intruding at this late hour, but I must speak to you. I'm afraid time is running short for both of us."

Biddle straightens. "The war?"

"It is not going well."

Biddle does a quick check of the area, letting out a breath of relief that no one is around. Then he takes Ferdek's arm and leads him into the consulate. Watcowski follows Biddle into the richly appointed office. The flowers are fresh with a spicey fragrance. Tasteful oil painting boasts the local countryside. Ferdek settles into the soft leather seat beside the uncluttered desk, while Biddle slides into his desk chair.

"I hear a lot of rumors, Ferdek. Is it true that your cavalry attacked a German Panzer unit riding horses?

The ambassador has trouble as his voice is cracking. "The charge was a brave one, though certainly ill-advised. The Germans slaughtered our brave boys."

Biddle leans forward, hands on his desk, a frown on his face. "What can we do to help you?"

"I'm afraid it is too late for anyone to help us. You have been a good friend, Anthony, as has your country. But this is our war because Germany attacked. We'll do what we have to do, alone."

Biddle straightens with resolve as he clears his throat. "My country will not forsake you at a time like this."

Ferdek, wishing he hadn't come, recognizes the hopeful tone. Shaking his head slowly, he replies, "Come now, Anthony. We both know your country will not go to war against Germany because Poland is standing in Hitler's way. Your country has to protect their interest first."

Biddle frowns, sensing the graveness of the remaining time in Poland. "How can Poland fight Germany alone?"

"How can anyone fight Germany? Their tanks own the ground. Their planes own the skies. They fight a war that strikes like a lightning bolt. We will fight or die and win or lose alone, Anthony. I am only here tonight to warn you that you, your staff, and the Americans in Poland need to escape while you can still find safe passage home. If you wait until the end of the week, it will be too late.

Biddle slaps his desk and shouts, "We won't leave you, Ferdek. Don't even think about it."

Ambassador Watcowski wearily stands to leave. He resolutely looks his diplomatic friend in the eye, fearing it will be for the last time. He straightens his shoulders. "You have only two choices, Anthony."

The U.S Ambassador waits in silence.

"You can go. Or you can leave your blood with mine on the streets of Warsaw.

Now very saddened, Biddle softly asks, "What about you, Ferdek?"

Ferdek heaves a heavy sigh. "My decision must not be made in the darkness of night but in the light of a new day. Tomorrow, we will all know. Tonight, I'm not at all sure."

Chapter 7

It is early evening in Gdansk. Ferdek, Tavius, and Wolfgang eye the armory from their vantage point as they lie flat atop a freight car. A German sentry marches past the door visible in the faint moonlight, holding his rifle tightly with his eyes searching the darkness. Their train moves unhurriedly down the track on a path just beyond the armory.

A German squad leader checks his watch, then looks up to acknowledge the engineer hanging out the window of the locomotive. Ferdek, Tavius, and Wolfgang roll off the top of the freight car and hit the ground roughly but silently. They use the train to shield them as they move quickly to the edge of a crumbling stone building. Ferdek looks up as a cloud eases across the moon to leave the land in total darkness. The clock in the watchtower shows twelve minutes until midnight. They acknowledge one another before checking the activity at the armory. They wait for the two German sentries to walk past the door, with nearly thirty seconds between them.

In low, hushed tones, Tavius states, "The guards pass every four minutes, give or take a minute or two."

Ferdek growls, "We don't have a minute or two leeway to get in and out. The timing must be accurate down to the second."

Wolfgang sarcastically offers, "You want me to go explain it to the guard? How do you expect us to be accurate down the second when they are stopping to take a sip of schnapps, relieve themselves, or flirt with some lady friend they have stashed on the other side of the armory?"

Sighing with frustration, Ferdek orders, "When the next guard passes, Tavius and I will go in. We'll have four minutes to find the vault, open it with the code Agata gave us, and get out with Baby."

Wolfgang questions, "I thought the plan was for all three of us to go in."

Ferdek continues, "The plan just changed. If we're not out in four minutes, eliminate the next guard who passes. That will give us eight minutes."

Alarmed, Wolfgang petitions, "Ferdek, what if you're not out in eight minutes?"

"Run like the demons of hell are after you because they will be. We won't be coming out.

Tavius tries to adapt to the new plan. "How many German sentries do you think are inside?"

Still studying the guard movement, Ferdek tersely replies, "Agata said three men would be guarding the vault."

Tavius nods, "We can take care of three men."

"Then there's the X factor."

Wide-eyed, Tavius asks, "What's that?"

"We don't know how many German soldiers are guarding the three sentries."

A sentry passes the door. Ferdek checks his pistol. "When he rounds the corner, we hit the door. I hope you can still pick locks."

"When we were boys, I kept us in candy picking locks."

"We're not after candy tonight."

As the German sentry rounds the corner and disappears, Ferdek whispers, "It's time."

Ferdek and Tavius run low through the ruined buildings to the door of the armory. The three-story structure built in the last century is designed for storage with a wide stairway in the center and rooms around the perimeter. Breathing heavily, Tavius works on the lock as Ferdek checks his watch. He looks nervously around the area.

The seconds tick away, but the lock doesn't open. Tavius drops his pick, and it falls to the ground. Nearly frantic, he uses his fingers to rake the dirt, searching for the pick. "Damn."

Ferdek is distracted by Tavius pawing around the ground. "What's wrong?"

"Can't find the pick."

A flashlight beam suddenly hits the ground where their attention is focused. Ferdek jerks his head up and stares into the face of a German. Ferdek slams his flashlight against the sentry's head and rams his elbow into the man's nose. Blood spurts, and the sentry crumbles to the ground.

Wolfgang runs to the sentry, grabs his legs, and begins dragging him away. In a low voice, Wolfgang laments, "Couldn't warn you. He would have heard me."

After grabbing the sentry's helmet and putting it on, Ferdek observes, "No longer matters."

Keeping the commotion to a minimum, Wolfgang drags the unconscious sentry behind the crumbling ruins.

Tavius, at last, grabs his pick from the dirt. "Found it."

Ferdek is conscious of time. "You have two minutes and fourteen seconds before the next sentry joins us. Maybe less."

Tavius smiles confidently as the lock clicks and the door swings open for them.

Ferdek and Tavius cautiously step into the dark abyss of the armory with only basic architectural knowledge of this type of structure. The men move stealthily toward the foot of the stairway in the middle of the room.

Once they are in place, Ferdek barks sharply and in German. "We have a problem."

As expected, a guard appears at the top of the stairs. A faint glow from the open door behind him shines muted light down the stairs. He demands, "What's happening down there?"

Ferdek hurries toward the door. In the darkness with the German helmet on his head, he looks like a soldier. He says, "Polish Partisans are trying to break into the armory."

A bit excited, the guard asks, "Where are they der Kamerad?"

"Behind the first line of trees. We have lost three men. They strike like ghosts, then vanish in the darkness. We need your help."

The guard, gripping his rifle with both hands, clomping his heavy boots on the wooden stairs, rushes to assist his comrades. Tavius springs the trap after the last stair is cleared and grabs the guard from behind. He silently slashes the soldier's throat with a knife. Ferdek catches the guard's rifle before it hits the floor. He looks at Tavius, standing above the slain guard, blood dripping off the knife's blade.

Ferdek quietly recounts, "Two more guards upstairs."

"Unless Agata was wrong."

"She's been right so far."

Smiling slightly, Tavius continues, "Then the odds are getting better all the time."

The two men ease their way up the stairs as if on tiptoe. The only light is a moonbeam slicing through a crack in an upstairs window. At the top of the stairs, Ferdek nods toward the corridor. "Third door on the left."

"Who goes in first?"

Ferdek holds up the rifle in the moonlight. "I have the firepower if we need it. Follow me."

"Fire that rifle, and we'll have to fight Hitler's Third Brigade to get Baby out safe and sound."

Ferdek and Tavius sneak down the hallway and stop at the third door on the left. Ferdek presses his ear against the panel. He holds up two fingers.

Tavius asks, "Footsteps?"

"Voices."

Ferdek steps back and crashes through the door startling a guard casually leaning on his rifle next to the vault. Ferdek spins around as he slams the butt of his rifle against the side of the solder's face sending him to the floor.

Tavius has his arm wrapped around the second German guard's neck, then swiftly and silently shoves his knife into the man's kidney. The second German guard slumps to the floor.

Ferdek sweeps his eyes along the wall, searching for the next piece of the puzzle. His gaze falls upon the painting of a fat and ugly naked woman on the far side of the room. He steps over the two fallen German guards and walks to the painting. He lifts it away from the wall. He reaches behind the canvas and turns with a broad grin, holding the key.

Ferdek tosses the key to Tavius, who then inserts the key into the vault, and the door swings open. Ferdek stares at a large package wrapped tightly with black cloth. After an eternity of a few seconds, he removes the package and gazes reverently at it.

"Say hello to Baby."

"It's not as large as I thought it would be."

"But just as deadly. It's time to take Baby home." Ferdek takes the package and gingerly places it in his backpack. The men move cautiously across the floor, past the window.

Tavius glances through the window and stops abruptly. "We have trouble." Ferdek joins him to look out the window. He frowns.

A German sentry stands beside Wolfgang, the barrel of his rifle jammed against Wolfgang's head.

Moonlight illuminates the desperate scene unfolding below. Wolfgang is on his knees. Squad members, with rifles in hand, are staring toward the second-floor window.

Tavius presses his back against the wall and questions, "You have an exit plan, I presume?"

Assessing the grim scene below, Ferdek stands in silence for a long beat. Then the exit plan comes with, "When I give you the word, shoot the sentry guarding Wolfgang."

Tavius alarmed then demands, "What if he kills our friend?"

Ferdek pragmatically states, "It is the chance Wolfgang will have to take."

Tavius angrily denounces, "You're not giving him a voice in the matter."

"The loss of one life is not as critical as moving Baby out of here. Wolfgang would be the first to tell you that."

Tavius is resigned to acceptance. "Only one thing's for certain."

"What?"

"He will die."

"Maybe we will all die."

Sighing, Tavius kneels beside the window. He opens it wide enough for the barrel of his rifle, still concealed in the darkness.

Keeping to the shadows, Ferdek crawls through the doorway. Hurrying to the top of the stairs, he removes his backpack and clutches it to his chest. He loudly barks, "Now!"

One gunshot rings out from the upstairs room, then a volley of loud voices erupt from outside the armory. Ferdek methodically removes a German grenade from his backpack. He looks over his shoulder to silently alert Tavius of the next phase.

Tavius has pulled away from the window, then dares to glance outside. A dead German sentry lies across Wolfgang's body. A dozen members of the squad are moving toward the armory entrance. Another sentry fires round after round toward the upstairs' window and Tavius.

Ferdek lays at the top of the stairs. After pulling the pin, he rolls the grenade and watches it drop down the staircase, step by step.

Ferdek mentally implores the weapon to continue its journey down the stairs.

The front door shakes.

The grenade rolls down to the next step.

The door flies open.

The grenade keeps rolling, one step at a time.

A German officer bolts into the armory, holding his pistol high, his eyes piercing the darkness.

The grenade falls one step at a time.

The sentry squad pushes into the armory.

The grenade decends, one step at a time.

The German officer motions his squad using his pistol toward the stairs.

The grenade tumbles relentlessly, one step at a time.

The squad reaches the stairs just as the grenade stops.

The squad moves up the stairs.

One soldier spots the grenade, points, and starts to scream. The grenade explodes, and the stairs crumble in a wild roar of flames that engulf the area. Wood splinters from the stairs become lethal projectiles for those not killed in the blast. The angry fire finishes the grim task.

Chapter 8

Outside the Royal Castle in Warsaw, the early morning traffic inches along like a race of snails. Pedestrians hurry down the sidewalk. A man stops at a newsstand to buy a paper. He scans the headlines anxiously, looking for hope, but then shakes his head with acceptance. A little girl exits an apartment and sits on the top step with a gray kitten. The people are solemn, each with their thoughts laced with fears of the future.

Inside his office, Ambassador Watcowski paces back and forth in front of his desk in his formal attire. Patrycja, faced etched with worry and uncertainty, enters without knocking. She is aristocratic and proper, but tears stain her cheeks. She wipes them quickly away and forces a brave smile.

"Father, you are dressed quite handsomely today. Are you expecting diplomatic visitors?"

Sadness crosses his usually bright, sparkling eyes. "No, my little Patrycja. They are content to wait for my funeral."

Wincing at his words, the ambassador gives Patrycja a stack of papers as she sits down behind the desk.

"These notes must be typed and then hand-delivered to the foreign secretaries before they get on the last plane to London."

"And what will you do, Father?"

"I will remain with my people until they are all gone, and Hitler stands at my door."

"We have not fallen to the Germans yet, Father. Our people will fight to the last man."

"Yes, my little Patrycja," he wearily replies. "We will fight to the last man, and then the Germans will kill the last man."

Patrycja juts out her defiant chin. "As long as we are alive, we have hope."

The ambassador angrily barks, "Our diplomatic corps is in shambles. Our army completely routed, and here I am trying to chronicle the last two weeks for—I don't know who will be left to read them. I don't know if anyone will ever read them. I guess I just want to tell our side of the story in case Poland ever exists again."

Patrycja slams a fist on the desk. "No matter how black things look at this moment, I promise you Poland will be back as a free country. We will not allow ourselves to be slaves to any invader."

The ambassador sits down on the edge of the desk. He can't help smiling in appreciation of his daughter's fierce assertion of Poland's right to sovereignty. "From my brief discussion with the German Ambassador, we know that Germany launched three full armies at Poland on September first." He looks down at a calendar on his desk as he circles September 3. At the top, the year boldly touts 1939.

"That was three days ago. The attack, initially scheduled for August twenty-sixth, for some reason, was postponed. It was our last five days of peace. I believe the invasion delay is because Germany is fearful that a full-scale attack may draw our allies, France, and Great Britain, into the fight.

Patrycja sneers with disgust and throws her pencil across the room. "Poland's allies? Does Germany think we have allies? Father, you have been pleading with them to prepare for the inevitable conflict with Germany since the armies of Der Fuhrer waltzed into Austria.

He muses aloud. "Maybe the invasion of Poland will finally open their eyes. Maybe they will realize that Germany may have their countries in the crosshairs of Hitler's mad dream."

"Father, not one finger was lifted by any of them when Great Britain refused to fight and gave

Czechoslovakia to Hitler without a shot fired, or a drop of blood spilled. I've had more trouble getting groceries from the market than the Germans have had with their land grabs. We would have been better off going to the Soviet Union for help."

The ambassador shakes his head. "I tried that. They have been unusually quiet of late, I fear, my little Patrycja, that Germany wants to lay waste to our lands, and Russia wants to steal and abolish everything good about Poland. Neither would be concerned if our names were erased forever from the maps of Europe."

Chapter 9

It's early morning in Gdansk. Ferdek, Tavius, and Wolfgang make their way quietly down an alley still untouched by the morning sun. They reach the sidewalk and stop at the sound of marching soldiers on worn cobblestone streets. They press their backs against the walls hoping the shadows will hide them while they wait for the soldiers to pass.

The three men are stunned to see twelve German soldiers marching Agata down the street. Her head is held high in defiance, even with her hands tied with rough rope behind her back. A Gestapo agent walks nonchalantly behind the soldiers. Agata is pushed roughly to the wall of the train station.

Tavius exclaims under his breath. "My, God!"

Wolfgang continues, "They're going to kill her."

Tavius rips their rifle from Ferdek's hand and aims with its barrel resting atop a garbage can. Ferdek places his hand on the rifle barrel and gently pushes it to the side and downward. His face is cut and streaked with blood from the mission in the armory.

Wolfgang cannot speak, but Tavius juts his chin and protests, "We just can't stand here and let her die."

Ferdek solemnly offers, "We have no other choice."

Wolfgang joins the protest, "But we wouldn't have Baby if it weren't for Agata."

Still watching the scene unfold, Ferdek continues, "We are all condemned to die the day we are born. Agata is a woman most fortunate."

Tavius, physically hurting and angry, states, "How can you say that?"

"Agata is dying for Poland."

Wolfgang raises his rifle in solidarity as he proclaims, "Then we shall all die for Poland today."

Ferdek reasons with his comrades. "Most likely, we will die, Wolfgang. But today is not that day. We have the secret for Poland's survival. We cannot throw it away because we are foolish enough to throw our lives away.

The argument ceases as shots rip through the air. Ferdek, Tavius, and Wolfgang return their gaze to the scene where smoke curls from the muzzles of German rifles. Agata sinks to the earth in a pool of blood. She twitches once, then is motionless. The men watch bitterly as the Gestapo agent smiles approvingly.

The soldiers march away, and the morning is silent again. Ferdek motions to his friends, and they scurry over the cobblestones to continue through the train yard. Wolfgang holds tightly to Tavius's arm as he limps over the track. They are momentarily distracted by the sound of voices singing and glance over their shoulders. It is a touching scene to see a handful of merchants from Gdansk, primarily old and gray, cross the street, singing an old funeral dirge. They surround the body of Agata. Two men stoop down and gently pick her up. They turn, still singing, and carry her across the street.

Tavius motions the others toward an empty boxcar. Ferdek stops short of getting in and stares down the track where German soldiers meticulously search each boxcar. Soldiers are boarding passenger trains.

Ferdek motions to his friends to join him. "We'll have to find another way out of Gdansk."

"You think they're looking for us?" asks Tavius.

Wolfgang interjects, "They're likely looking for Baby and will execute anybody who has it."

Tavius bitterly laughs. "Then I guess they're looking for us, and I'm sure they have roadblocks on every road out of town."

There is a roar overhead. A squadron of German planes blots out the sky.

Wolfgang resignedly states, "So much for hiding in the woods."

Tavius brightly offers, "We may be the most wanted men in Poland, and you can't say that about most thieves."

Ferdek laughs at the absurdity of their circumstances. "Thieves steal loaves of bread because they are hungry. We're criminals of the highest order. We stole Baby."

Wolfgang continues, "They'll shoot us on sight if they find us."

Tavius nods. "But we may win the war if they don't."

The three weave their way among the trains, keeping out of sight, moving across an open field. They hear the drone of a plane. Simultaneously the men drop to the ground, hugging the earth until the sound of the aircraft dies in the distance.

It's midday, and the trio has made good progress as they crawl through the grass out of the woodlands. They've made it to an old bridge that crosses a river. The trouble is they are not the only ones ready to cross the river.

A squad of German soldiers crosses the bridge. They stop to look down at the water below them. Two soldiers climb back onto the bridge. The German soldiers pick up the pace and run off the bridge and down an old dirt road.

The bridge erupts in a fiery bomb explosion. As the smoke clears, several German tanks advance to the far side of the river, spreading out in a wall of metal and firepower. Ferdek, Tavius, and Wolfgang feel their spirits evaporating in the smokey destruction.

Ferdek lowers his binoculars to focus on the sound of a plane flying overhead. He glances up. "They have us cut off." He pulls a wrinkled map from his pocket and spreads it out on the ground. He uses his fingers to trace the roads and rivers leaving Gdansk. "We're either a day too late, or the Germans arrived a day too early. They will no doubt be waiting for us at every possible escape route I've marked. They know we're here. They know what we've stolen. They want it back."

Wolfgang offers, "Poland is a big land."

"Not big enough. We can hide for a while, Wolfgang, but not forever."

Tavius laments, "If we don't get Baby home, it might as well still be in German hands. The Brits and the French won't last a month. They have one chance for survival."

Wolfgang adds, "Still, Baby is trapped with us."

Tavius nods. "And we're stuck out here in no man's land."

Ferdek suddenly grins. "That's it."

Wolfgang frowns. "What's it?"

Ferdek continues, "They're out here searching for us, and we're going to where no one's looking for us, where no one expects us to be."

Tavius looks puzzled. "Where's that?"

"We get lost in Gdansk."

Wolfgang and Tavius both stared at their friend, fearing the stress has reduced him to the Mad Hatter from Wonderland. "We drink beer where the soldiers drink beer."

Wolfgang squints, searching for sanity. "You have a death wish, Ferdek?"

"Would rabbits who escaped a wolf's lair be foolish enough to go back?"

Tavius promises, "Only if they wanted to die."

"The wolf knows the faces of the rabbits but the only Germans who know our faces died at the armory."

Wolfgang shrugged. "So, we wait?"

"Like boys who'd rather drink their beer than fight."

"For how long?" Tavius wonders.

Without answering, Ferdek looks again toward the river through his binoculars. A tank turns its gun toward the woodlands and fires. Flames and smoke pour out of the barrel. The men feel the heat and vibration from the whistle of the shot overhead.

Ferdek lowers his binoculars. "Until the Germans tire of looking for us. After a few days, maybe they'll think: the boys are gone; the boys are dead; Baby is lost. Baby may be at the bottom of the river. Baby will die of rust. They will then turn their army toward Warsaw.

Wolfgang presses, "And where will we be?"

Ferdek answers, "Already in Warsaw."

Tavius still concerned about the logistics. "Just how do we get there?"

Ferdek winks. "One step at a time, Tavius. One step at a time."

Wolfgang focused on the German military arms. "What if the tank shoots again? In this direction?"

Tavius chuckles. "Stay low, Wolfgang. The German is shooting high."

The three men crawl through the fragrant tall, damp grass back toward the woodlands.

Chapter 10

The day is gray and overcast in Gdansk. A Grosser Mercedes touring car eases down the street. Pedestrians stand solemnly on the sidewalk and watch the car pass by with fear and resentment. The Nazi flags mounted on the two front fenders have a chilling effect on the fearful citizens.

The touring car stops at the front steps and gray columns of the German military headquarters. Police General Friedrich-Georg Eberhardt steps from the vehicle and glances left, right, front, and back. His face is stern, carved from granite. His eyes are just as hard and demanding. After a contemptuous look at the men, he climbs the steps while his military escorts follow.

Inside the Nazi headquarters, Lieutenant Wilhelm Henningsen sits beside his aide at a long conference table. Lying in front of him is a map of Gdansk and its surrounding countryside.

The door opens, spilling the morning light into the room, and Henningsen glances up as General Eberhardt swaggers defiantly and alone into the room. Henningsen and his aide snap to attention and salute. Eberhardt acknowledges the salutes with a nod and a wave; then, he plops down heavily at the table. Henningsen and his aide continue to stand, visibly apprehensive.

General Eberhardt speaks slowly but deliberately. "We have a situation. Please sit down, Lieutenant, and tell me what you're going to do to solve the problem that confronts both of us in Gdansk."

Henningsen accepts the invitation to sit, but his aide remains standing. "We'll capture them, General."

Eberhardt raises an eyebrow in disbelief and asks, "Do you know where they are?"

Henningsen eyes his aide and uncomfortably admits, "They've fled Gdansk."

Eberhardt was growing agitated. "Are you certain?"

Henningsen pauses then swallows. "Our soldiers spotted them down beside the railroad tracks."

Even more deliberate, Eberhardt demands, "Were they shot?"

Henningsen squirms in his seat. "Our orders were to capture them."

Eberhardt presses, "Did you?"

Henningsen, no longer capable of eye contact with the General, quietly replies, "We lost them in a crowd that had gathered to witness the execution of a Polish spy."

Eberhardt stares out the window, clenching and unclenching his jaws. He is not happy. "How many are there?"

"Three, sir."

Eberhardt demands through clenched teeth. "And how were they able to steal the gadget?"

Henningsen relates, "We had it locked in a vault in the old armory. Someone must have given them the combination to the lock."

In a low growl, Eberhardt asks, "Who?"

Henningsen resigned to his fate states, "The spy who we executed at the railroad station."

Eberhardt is still not satisfied raises his voice. "Why weren't the thieves stopped at the armory?"

"Our men had them pinned down, sir."

Eberhardt's breathing is short due to aggravation and the rage rising on his face. "And who let them get away?"

"The men, sir."

"What about them?"

"They are all dead, sir."

Eberhardt slams his fist to the top of the table. His face is white with rage, and his eyes are burning with anger. "Are you telling me that a whole squad of our finest fighting men could not stop three men?"

"That's the report I received."

Eberhardt stands and paces back and forth beside the table. He abruptly stops. "Your orders have changed, Lieutenant.

"Yes, sir."

General Eberhardt is barely in control of his rage. "Find them. I don't care how many men it takes. Scour every inch of Poland if you have to but find them."

"Yes, sir."

Eberhardt orders, "Shoot them on sight." To emphasize his meaning, Eberhardt whirls with his pistol in his hand and fires one shot. The bullet hits the aide above his right eye, and the aide crumbles to the floor. Henningsen stares at the dead man. There is no doubt of the price of failing this general.

Eberhardt finally back in control of his breathing. "Bring me the gadget when you do. I will not tolerate failure a second time."

Eberhardt strides to the door. He pulls it open and walks out of the room. The echo after he slams it behind reverberates around the lieutenant. Henningsen is still staring at the dead man. It is only the fact that he's in near shock that keeps his stomach from ejecting its contents.

Chapter 11

In the morning in the countryside just outside of Gdansk, all is quiet. Ferdek rises from behind a pile of grain and sprints, keeping low to the ground, toward the barn. He steps inside, blinking his eyes, adjusting to the darkness. As his eyes adjust, he takes note of a cow standing in the far corner, tied with a rope to a post. Hay litters the floor, and a wooden ladder leads to the loft, which appears to be empty. Sunlight filters through a single, dirty window. He walks to the window and waves his hand down the glass pane. Moments later, Tavius and Wolfgang burst through the door, out of breath, their faces strained but pleased to have a place to rest.

Ferdek states, "We can hide here 'til dark."

Wolfgang asks, "What if the farmer finds us?"

Tavius offers, "He's Polish. He won't turn us out and leave us to the mercy of the Germans."

Wolfgang unconvinced. "What if he's a spy?"

Ferdek looks unconcerned. "We'll deal with it either way."

Wolfgang muses, "He might think we're thieves."

Laughing and holding up the backpack containing Baby, Ferdek offers, "He might be right."

Tavius asks, "What do we do the rest of the day?"

Ferdek casually suggests, "Sit, and wait, and hope the Germans are looking for us elsewhere."

Tavius sarcastically replies, "Hope is not a plan. They know what we've done by now. They can't afford to let us escape. They'll be looking under every rock to find us."

Wolfgang brightly offers, "Then we are a lucky bunch of bastards."

Puzzled, Ferdek asks, "What makes you say that?"

Chuckling, Wolfgang retorts, "Poland has a lot of rocks."

The constant danger with almost no sleep is catching up to the men. Wolfgang and Tavius drop to the floor, their backs against the wall with their eyes on the barn door. Ferdek stares in silence through the window. All he sees are the grasses rippling in the wind. The daylight slowly fades to dark.

Fight as they try, sleep overtakes the weary men. As the afternoon drifts into the evening, the three drift farther into a much-needed slumber.

There is a distinctive sound of a metallic click. Ferdek snaps to a fully awake state. Even though it's dark in the barn, his eyes open wide at the barrels of five rifles aimed at him. Ferdek slides to a sitting position and raises his arms. "Who are you?"

The response is the silent rifles pointed toward his heart. Hoping for mercy, Ferdek searches eyes of the faces but sees souls willing to fight first and ask questions later. Illuminated by moonlight from the window, there is an eeriness in the faces of them all.

Ferdek tries to earn some trust. "We were only looking for a place to spend the night. I heard a storm's coming. We'll be gone by first light and won't take a thing with us when we go."

Tavius and Wolfgang are rapidly rousting themselves from their deep sleep. Trying some good-natured comments to these people as he wipes the grit from his eyes, Tavius proclaims, "I'll even feed the cow before I go."

Wolfgang grins. However, no one else does, so his grin fades. The men's tenseness grows in the oppressive silence.

Halina pushes two of the men aside and stands in front of Ferdek. She wears a wicked smile as she defiantly folds her arms across her chest. "I told you earlier that you would need a girl before you left Gdansk."

"I don't understand."

"Do you remember me?"

It is Wolfgang who replies, "I couldn't forget you if I tried."

Halina rebukes, "You turned me down."

Wolfgang unflinchingly proclaims, "You are only a girl."

Halina reaches into her jacket pocket and removes a Kongsberg colt. She kneels and jams the pistol between Wolfgang's eyes. "It's been a long time since I was a girl."

Wolfgang firmly replies, "You're no older than eighteen."

"I killed my first man when I was fifteen. I may kill my next man tonight. But I am a woman now. The Germans gave me no choice. A girl grows up quick, or she doesn't grow up at all."

Halina's statement seems to have calmed her. She stands and holds the pistol loosely at her side.

Ferdek struggles to understand their position. "What do you want with us? If you want money, we have little. You can take it." Ferdek pulls a handful of change from his pocket and gives it to Halina.

The leader Mizella, the oldest man, strikes Ferdek's hand with the barrel of his rifle, sending the coins flying across the barn floor. Contention flares in his eyes. "Do not offend us, young man! We are here to help you. But we can just as easily bury you in the ground so far away from your mother, bless her soul, will never be able to find you, and the wolves will suck your bones and leave fragments from here to Warsaw."

"We have been watching you since the moment you arrived." Halina adds, "We did not know why you were in Gdansk or what you were doing here, but we knew it must be important."

Tavius, alarmed at her comment, cautiously corrects, "You must have us mistaken for someone else."

Wolfgang chimes in hastily. "We were simply on our way home when night caught us." Almost on queue, thunder echoes in the distance, soon followed by flashes of lightning that dance outside the window.

Halina is unconvinced. "The Germans want you dead."

Mizella continues, "They have been tracking you like wild dogs all day. Word on the streets of Gdansk says you stole something significant to the Nazis. They want it back. They catch you, and they will not negotiate. They want your blood to ooze into Polish soil.

Ferdek innocently asks, "What is it we are supposed to have stolen?"

Annoyed that the men are so cagey, Halina mocks, "We don't know."

Mizella states, "We don't care what it is. Maybe it's a bomb. Perhaps it's far worse. Possibly it will kill us all before morning. But if the Germans want it, and the Germans fear it, then we want to make sure you reach your destination before a German bullet finds you.

Ferdek climbs to his feet and dusts himself off. He shifts his gaze from Halina to Mizella.

Tavius questions, "What makes you believe you can help us?"

Halina proudly states, "We are gypsies. Germans know the roads to here, there, and just about everywhere. We travel the trails where no roads have ever gone. Some say we are like ghosts. We come. We go. No one ever knows we were there."

Ferdek acknowledges, "Like tonight. I didn't hear you, and even in my sleep, I was listening for anything that might not sound right."

Halina pleased, shares a wink. "We are one with the darkness. We appear when we want to be seen."

Wolfgang probes, "Why would you want to help us?"

Mizella offers, "You believe you can defeat the Germans. We believe it's an impossible quest. But if there is a one in a hundred chance you can, we want to be a part of your success. We may be gypsies. We may never stay in any one place long enough to plant roots. But Poland is our home, too. It may take us forever, but we swear by the Mother of God that we will erase every footprint the Germans leave on our soil."

Thunder rumbles in the distance, and they all cringe. It sounds like cannon fire.

Chapter 12

It's early morning in the woodlands with a light fog blanketing over the area. A gypsy caravan of three wagons eases through the timber and down a hill toward a river. Wolfgang sits with Halina. She holds the reins and guides the horses through the forest. While they both stare straight ahead, Wolfgang asks, "What will the Germans do to you if they catch you smuggling us out of Gdansk?"

Halina fixed her gaze. "First, they must find us."

"But what if they do?"

Halina shrugs in resolution like a hunter with no options. "They will kill us and burn our wagons, then pretend we never existed at all. We are like cockroaches beneath the heels of their boots. They want to cleanse the land of Jews and Gypsies alike. In the eyes of the Nazis, we don't have the God-given right to breathe the same air they do."

"Then we must part company."

"Why do you say that?"

Wolfgang nods toward the river. She spots the Nazi war machine peeking over the ridge, the motley green camouflage paint appearing stark against the land. The turrets identify the ominous formidable line of tanks, knowing the cannons and soldiers would appear as well. Halina stops the wagon, turns back, and waves for the other two wagons to pause as well.

Mizella walks nonchalantly to Halina's wagon. "Do you see what we see?"

Smiling, Mizella exchanges like a sage survivor to a youngster with respect. "I wonder if there are any Germans left in Germany or if they have all come to Poland."

Halina clenches her jaws and removes her Kronesberg colt pistol from her jacket pocket. Mizella gently places his hand on the gun and pushes it into her lap. "It would be a short fight, dear Halina. There will come a time when we must take a stand, but today is not the day.

"Where will we run?"

"Straight ahead."

"Dead into the Nazi soldiers?"

"It's too late to run anywhere else. A mad dash across Poland would only kill our horses. Besides, we have the one critical weapon the Germans don't have."

"What's that?"

"We have the river, Halina."

Mizella soon has the men down from the wagons explaining the situation. Ferdek, Tavius, and Wolfgang stand beside the lead wagon, all with solemn faces as they listen to the options.

Ferdek speaks up. "What choices do we have?"

Tavius offers, "We can hide in the thickets."

Mizella frowns then sourly comments, "The Nazis will cut you down."

Wolfgang looks on bravely. "It's too late to run."

Mizella adds, "There's no place to go. Germans are ahead of you. Germans are behind you. Poland is in a vice, squeezed on all sides by the Germans."

Ferdek confesses, "We don't want to endanger you or your family, Mizella. You've done everything you could to help us. If the Germans find out, you'll be dead before the Nazis have their noon meal. We're on our own now."

Ferdek turns to walk away. Mizella grabs him by his shoulder. "I have a plan."

Tavius quickly leans forward. "Let's hear it."

"You won't like it," Mizella replies.

Ferdek leans in, encouraging the discussion. "Will it take us to the far side of the German army?"

Confidently Mizella grins. "It will." Mizella looks out toward the river and the advancing German war machine. "If you survive."

Within minutes Ferdek is spread-eagle, his hands tied with ropes to the bottom staves of the wagon.

Tavius similarly positioned underneath the second wagon bottom. As his legs get secured to the rear axle of the wagon, his breathing elevates.

Wolfgang is under the third wagon. He presses his head against the bottom of the wagon. A rope is looped around his waist and then tied to a stave. Mizella is on his hands and knees, supervising the operation for each in turn.

Wolfgang uneasily comments. "What happens if the Germans search the bottom of the wagons?"

"They won't find you." Mizella confidently replies.

"What makes you so sure?"

Mizella rather pleased with his solution. "You, my boy, will be under water."

"We could drown before you reach the other side."

Mizella pulls a coin from his pocket, flips it in the air, and catches it without revealing the results. "It's fifty-fifty."

"The odds aren't good."

Mizella comments, "Those odds are as good as any of us get or can hope to have. Keep your mouth pressed hard against the bottom of the wagon, and you will find small air holes. The wind is good today. Ripples in the river will separate the water from the wagon. Breathe slowly, and don't panic. The river is not so wide here."

Mizella rises and starts to walk away. He stops abruptly and kneels again to look under the wagon, and smiles confidently. "One other thing."

"What's that?"

Mizella smirks slightly. "I am not a religious man, but if I were tied to the bottom of a wagon crossing the river, I would pray."

Chapter 13

The morning sun embraces the area revealing all the foliage and colors. The caravan moves slowly out of the woodlands and toward the River Vistula.

A German rowboat crosses the river to meet the gypsies. Mizella holds the reins, and Halina is sitting beside him, a robe lying across her lap. The wagon stops at the banks of the river. The German rowboat reaches shore just as the caravan eases axle-deep into the water.

Lieutenant Henningsen steps out of the boat and wades with hurried steps toward the lead wagon followed by a dozen men, all armed with rifles held chest high. Henningsen is ankle-deep in the water while Mizella remains seated. Each stares at one another with contempt and defiance.

Henningsen, with a smug look of self-worth, commands, "You seem to have lost your way."

Mizella reservedly offers, "This is my country, sir. I know it as well as the smile on my wife's lips."

Henningsen points to Halina with a smirk. "Your wife?"

"My daughter."

Henningsen assesses the two with contempt. "Where are you coming from?"

"Koszwaly."

"What were you doing in Koszwaly?"

"We sell things."

"What kinds of things?"

Mizelle opens his features to the possibilities with dancing eyes and upturned lips. "Fortunes told. Palms read. Charms. Rings. Golden amulets to ward off the evil eyes. Beautiful hand-woven robes." He points to Halina.

Halina stands with a smile, showing off the robe in her lap, letting the robe fall around her feet. Henningsen does not look impressed. "Where is your destination?"

"The town of Kalisz."

"What do you have waiting in Kalisz?"

"Family."

Henningsen smirks as if he has caught a weasel in a trap. "I thought Gypsies were nomads."

"My mother owns a dress shop in Kalisz. I'm afraid I was the only wayward nomad.

"I think you are lying."

"Does it really matter?"

Henningsen ignores the words of the gypsy. He pulls a map of Poland from his briefcase and presses against the side of the wagon. "How close did you travel to Gdansk?"

Mizella shows disdain across his face and spits over the side into the water. "We gave Gdansk a wide berth. There is a war going on, and we are peaceful people. I have heard that there is a lot of fighting in the streets of Gdansk. No one is buying. No one is selling. We have chosen to go in another direction."

"Have you crossed paths with three young men fleeing Gdansk?"

Mizella slowly shakes his head. "We don't travel the roads, sir. We have seen no one, and I doubt if anyone, other than yourself, has seen us. But armies don't use the roads either, I see."

"Step down."

"Why?"

"If we search the wagons, what will we find?"

Mizella shrugs. "Maybe someone to read your palm, tell your fortune, or sell you a gold amulet to ward off the evil eye. Who knows what you will find?"

Mizella steps down and motions for the other drivers to step down as well. They do.

Ferdek has his face pressed against the bottom of the wagon. The level of the river has reached his ears, but he resolves to hang on.

German soldiers climb into each of the three wagons. Moments later, they crawl out and jump down. A sergeant walks briskly toward Henningsen and salutes.

"The wagons are empty, sir."

Henningsen frowns. "You didn't search for very long, sergeant."

"There was not a lot of space to search, sir."

"You are sure no one is hiding in the wagons?"

"The wagons are empty, sir."

Henningsen is disappointed. "Very well."

Henningsen looks up at Mizella. "If I find you have lied to me, I will track down you and your family like rabbits. And I can assure you that no one will ever see you again. No one will ever remember you were here."

The lieutenant turns and wades toward the waiting rowboat. Mizella and Halina solemnly watch as Henningsen climbs into the boat, and it turns toward the opposite shoreline.

Mizella motions everyone in his group to get back into the wagons. The caravan moves slowly out of the water and threads its way past the German tanks and soldiers. German soldiers shower Halina with catcalls as the lead wagon passes by. The soldiers hammer the butts of their rifles against the wagons. Others grab the wagons and rock them back and forth. The second wagon almost tips over but regains its balance. Mizella, Halina, and the gypsy drivers stare solemnly ahead.

Lieutenant Henningsen steps out of the rowboat onto the shore. He contemptuously watches the wagons move toward the timberline. In moments the wagons are swallowed up by nature and melt into the trees.

Verifying they are out of the Germans' line of sight Mizella reins for his horses to stop. He leaps to the ground and draws a long knife from his belt as he crawls under the lead wagon. The drivers of the other two wagons do the same.

Mizella slices the ropes around Ferdek's hands. Halina reaches his side and holds Ferdek's body in place while Mizella cuts the ropes around the young man's feet. Ferdek falls hard on the ground. He lies still, lifeless.

Halina places his head in her hands and softly calls, "Ferdek." There is no response, only silence.

Halina pleads while lifting his torso. "Ferdek, can you hear me? Ferdek, please answer me!"

Ferdek coughs, gasping for air. Water gushes from his chest as he coughs again and again.

Mizella grabs Ferdek's ankles and drags him from beneath the wagon. She turns him on his side as he regurgitates river water.

"Is he alright?" Halina begs with tears in her eyes.

Mizella laughs. "The boy's fine. He just tried to drink the river dry, that's all."

Mizella stands up and jams the knife into his belt. Halina races to the last wagon and holds Wolfgang's hands to steady him as he crawls out from the wagon. Ferdek forces himself into a sitting position. He glances toward the other two wagons. Tavius uses a wagon wheel to pull himself back onto his feet. Wolfgang walks on unsteady feet, Halina's arms support him. He is wiping water from his face and hair. Drenched to the bone, rivers of water run off each of them into mini pools at their feet.

Ferdek glances up at Mizella. "Did the Germans find Baby?"

Mizella shakes his head. "Baby is safe."

Halina glances over her shoulder at the wagon. "I had Baby at my feet the whole time. I even showed the robe to the German Lieutenant. He didn't have an interest, not even when I let the robe drop down around Baby.

Ferdek grins with relief. He pushes himself to his feet. "How can we repay you? We would not have made it without your help, Mizella."

"We do not ask for payment. We are Polish. Men like you and me never walk on the same side of the street, not where anyone can see us, but we both have great pride in our homeland.

Ferdek respectfully bows. "I will not forget you."

Halina asks, "You can tell me one thing before you go, Ferdek?"

"What's that?"

"What's Baby?"

Ferdek cagily grins. "If we win the war..."

"We will win the war," Mizella revises.

"...then you will have Baby to thank."

Halina reaches up and kisses Ferdek, and then Wolfgang on the cheek.

Halina softly offers, "Stay safe. I will miss you, but I would like to live a long life. I think you are a dangerous man."

Wolfgang smiles. "We just have a job to do, Miss Halina."

"Who dies?"

Wolfgang shakes his head slightly. "In war, we simply do what we must do, and we all die a little each day."

Chapter 14

Dusk wraps around the city of Warsaw like a mother swaddling her babe. The capital lies in darkness and shadows, with only a few lights burning in the approaching night. The view seems peaceful.

Ferdek, Tavius, and Wolfgang emerge from the forest and look down on their home.

Ferdek observes, "All is calm."

"The storm is coming," Tavius notes.

Wolfgang counters, "No, the storm is already here." He lifts his eyes to the far distance discerning German tank silhouettes on the plains north of town. Combat vehicles race back and forth along a line of soldiers and mobile artillery placements.

Tavius laments, "I didn't think the Germans would get here this quickly."

Ferdek states, "They figure to walk across Poland without facing any real resistance," Ferdek states, "bury us beneath their Nazi heels, and then move as rapidly as possible toward France and Great Britain."

Wolfgang barks, "They don't know the courage of the Polish, Ferdek."

"It has nothing to do with courage, Wolfgang. It's all about weapons. The Germans have them, and we don't."

"Then why are we fighting?" Tavius argues. "Why have we chosen to die for nothing?"

Ferdek stoically admits, "We can't save Poland. We can't stop the German army on Polish soil. It was too late, before the first shot. But we have an opportunity to make a difference. Admittedly it offers a small and improbable chance of stopping Germany before it crushes the rest of Europe."

Wolfgang's face soured like he had swallowed tainted meat. "That's a long shot, Ferdek."

"It's the only option we have."

Tavius asks, "So, you're determined to go through with this, Ferdek?"

"I am. But each man must make his own decision. I would not force you to go further but look how far we've come."

Wolfgang grins. "You're certainly not going anywhere without us."

Chapter 15

It's in the wee hours of the night. The streets are dark and silent as Ambassador Watcowski stands with Kondrat Mickelowski beside a fountain in Saski Park. In the distance, they hear car horns honk, a faraway police siren, and the steady rumble of traffic on the streets. Up close, the fountain gurgles and splashes, sounding incongruous to their ears. They sense a strange foreboding around them as they study the view.

Kondrat comments, "Warsaw is a beautiful city."

"The work of architects who were true artists."

"And now we are going to lose it."

"That, I'm afraid, is the ultimatum we face, Kondrat."

"What are you trying to say?"

"If we stay and fight to the last man, as my heart says we should do, the ages-old beauty of Warsaw will be destroyed down to the last brick. Bombs leave dreadful scars."

"And if we leave?"

"We save the beauty of Warsaw, but it will belong to those who don't see its beauty or love the city as you and I do, Kondrat."

"Will we ever be able to come home again?"

"We can when the war ends, but it won't be our home anymore."

"Mr. Ambassador, if you see my son before I do, please let him know that he must take our family out of Poland and to our chalet in Switzerland. He is young and strong. He will make sure they arrive safely."

"You can tell him yourself, Kondrat. Do not despair."

Kondrat stares at the ground and shakes his head. "None of us knows what lies in store for tomorrow. Perhaps we will all be able to go together. Perhaps we go separately. Perhaps we will meet again, you and I, Mr. Ambassador. But perhaps not. Man is not destined for this earth forever, and I hear the footsteps of death close behind me."

The ambassador begins walking away. "Are you coming with me, Kondrat?"

Kondrat shoulders hunch over like that of an older man as he fills with melancholy. "I think I'll stay here in the park for a while. It holds so many good memories for me. As long as I am here, they do not leave me."

Night yields to the early sunrise in Warsaw. Outside the Royal Castle, Poland's seat of government, the residents crowd the sidewalks, carrying their belongings in wagons and packed on their backs as they begin their escape from the German army. Inside the Royal Castle, the Polish Ambassador and Patrycja look out the window at the frantic crowd of people leaving town. They look up each time they hear the low rumble of artillery fire in the distance.

"It's terribly sad, Father. Many Poles built their lives here, and they were happy lives, often prosperous lives, but now they are fleeing for their lives."

"Weep for them, my little Patrycja, then weep for us all. Before the week is over, perhaps before the day ends, we will be down there with them. As they go, we will go. As they die, we perish behind them."

"No, Father. We will fight."

The ambassador hugs his daughter tightly. "No, Daughter, we will live to fight another day. If not us, then your children or their children will surely come back to Warsaw someday and remember us as the last generation who built a great city."

A loud ruckus in the ambassador's office interrupts their conversation. The ambassador and Patrycja turn as Ferdek, Tavius, and Wolfgang burst through the door. They appear weary with their hair disheveled and clothes streaked with dirt and mud. None of them have shaved for days. The strain and exhaustion permeate their bodies.

Patrycja runs to Ferdek and hugs him. She wipes the mud off his face with her handkerchief. "Where in the world have you been? I've been so worried about you, all of you. What happened? You look as if you crawled through the mud from there to here. I'm afraid even to ask where there was."

Ferdek takes her arms and pushes her gently away. A frustrated Ferdek announces, "Father, we've just come from Gdansk and saw the German army trying to encircle Warsaw. The word on the street is that the Polish marshal has ordered a general retreat. We're surrendering Warsaw."

Tavius and Wolfgang dejectedly seek the closest chairs, pausing to rest while Ferdek shares their quest.

"I know, my son. I was with him when the decision was made."

"Why didn't you try to stop him?"

"We have no army that can stop the Germans."

"Father, the time has come for Poland to stand and fight."

"Son, it is not the time to die. You were with the Pomorska Cavalry brigade, yes? Is it your intention to return to them and ask for your sword and lance?"

Ferdek turns away, his jaws clenched, his fists in tight balls. His eyes blaze with conviction. "I would rather die with honor than stand idly by like cowards and let Germany run roughshod over our homeland. We will never be Nazi slaves."

"We have one chance to survive this conflict, my son."

Ferdek numbly asks, "Run?"

"Do you plan to run back to your Pomorska Cavalry brigade? Is it your intention to ask for your sword and lance with a place in the front line? You can't go back and fight with your brigade, son. You have no brigade. It no longer exists. Your cavalry unit launched a very brave but very foolish charge at the Germans. They ran directly into the path of German panzers. Only God knows where you were when the order came to charge. But you are the only one still alive."

Ferdek collapses into a chair near his friends. His face the image of hurt, anger, and sorrow consumed with grief and shame. He fights the underlying resentment at an impossible situation. "There is more than one way to defeat the Germans."

Ferdek takes the backpack off his shoulder and clutches it in his arms.

Patrycja gently pats her brother's shoulder, trying to console him. She softly offers, "To fight at another time in another place, Ferdek, we first have to survive."

"The Germans are stronger than we are," Ferdek argues. "Their army is more powerful than ours but will not win because we will outsmart them."

Patrycja looks hopefully to the brother, her long-time protector. "You have a plan?"

Ferdek looks into her hopeful eyes, and a wicked grin erupts across his face. "We have the ultimate weapon."

Patrycja frowns, sensing he is tired from his long journey. "What is it?"

Ferdek holds his backpack over his head in triumph. "When the time is right, you'll know. The whole world will. We have the key to Germany's greatest secrets." The three young men grin.

Patrycja glances at her father. Both are puzzled.

Chapter 16

The afternoon sun is drifting toward evening in Warsaw. The stone façade of the Royal Castle, Poland's seat of government, is the only constant witness of Polish families clinging together as they continue their forced pilgrimage out of the city. Numb to most of the noise, they uniformly wince at the distant gunfire, like keeping time to the beat of a drum. Sirens wail in every direction as the castle door opens to have Ferdek, Tavius, and Wolfgang step out, followed by the ambassador and Patrycja.

Ferdek the elder, says, "Wolfgang, your father wants you to make sure your family gets out of Poland safely. He will allow my family to accompany you as long I can arrange suitable transportation for you all."

Wolfgang shakes his head. "Forgive me, sir, but I don't agree with your assessment of the situation."

Tavius defiantly adds, "Neither do I, sir. We are only two weeks into battle, and we are talking about our military, our government, and our people all turning their backs on our country."

"Where can we go?" Wolfgang asks. "How can we get there? German soldiers control the roads. They are circling Warsaw. They are cutting off every exit."

"Young men, from the reports I have received, you can take the road out of Warsaw to the southeast and stay clear of any military personnel. I want all of you to throw away your military uniforms and remain dressed in civilian clothes like peasants for the trip ahead of you. If caught in the uniforms of the Polish army, you'll be shot as deserters. If the Germans capture you, they will at least treat you like prisoners of war."

"At this point, I doubt it, Father. Germany wants our land. They want to see every Polish man, woman, and child, lying in a ditch or some shallow grave. They want to erase us from the face of the earth."

"What makes you say this, my son?"

"You haven't been in Gdansk the past few days and seen what we have seen taking place. Our contact was taken out and brutally murdered by a firing squad. No questions asked. No trial."

Looking horrified as he digested the possibilities and wrapping his arm around his daughter, he pulled her close. "What did he do to upset the Germans?"

Ferdek spits, "It wasn't he, Father. It was she."

"A spy?"

Ferdek remorsefully replies, "A Polish citizen and the daughter of your uncle."

Wolfgang, straightens towering over everyone, declares, "I have not yet agreed to my father's request. He raised me to be a man and not run when my gut instinct and my military training tells me I need to stay and fight."

"Wolfgang, your father raised you to be a good son. Your family needs you now. You cannot turn your back on them."

"There is no honor in running," Tavius solemnly states.

"If there is honor in dying, it is soon forgotten. What good is a headstone when the son is gone? Wolfgang, will you not take your parents and my daughter to safety? How do you think they will escape on their own?

Patrycja bristles. Her vivid green eyes flash with anger. "Who said I was leaving? I know how to shoot, Father. You taught me when I was much younger, and you taught me well. I have no intention of leaving. They may kill me next week or murder me before morning. But they will have to wade through the bodies of their dead to reach me. If I spill my blood, I will have it spilled on the ground of my ancestors."

The ambassador pulls her back closer with his arm around her shoulders but ignores her words. He turns to Ferdek and hands him an envelope. "You must deliver this letter to the airfield within the next two hours. The remaining members of our provisional government are on that plane, bound for Great Britain to join with the rest of the government. All of our naval resources have followed protocol and made their way to Great Britain."

Ferdek asks, "Who receives the letter?"

"Find Phillip Kandinsky. He will make sure it reaches Wladyslaw Sikorski, who will become our president and the commander-in-chief of our military."

"What has happened to President Moscicki?" Ferdek questions.

"He was forced to resign and has taken exile in Switzerland."

Ferdek is unwilling to let it drop. "What was his sin?"

"He was the only one in Warsaw who did not believe the Germans would begin their war on Poland."

Tavius walks to Patricia's side and takes her hand. "I know you are a fighter. I well understand the patriotic blood that flows in your veins. It flows in mine also. But I cannot permit you to stay in Warsaw under these dire circumstances. Allow me to accompany you and Ferdek on this errand. Although it grieves me greatly, I insist we follow your father's wise counsel."

The ambassador stands in silence, his face grim as he watches his Polish community struggle in their plight to escape a country being torn apart by war. He turned his back toward his hope for the future. "In addition to the Luftwaffe's intention to bomb our capital, I have been informed that there is a flanking move by the German XIX Corp around Warsaw to capture Brest Litovsk. There is a brave effort by the eighteenth Polish division to defend the city, but our army does not have the arsenal needed to stop the onslaught. The invading panzer troops are under the command of General Heinz Guderian."

They fall deathly silent, oblivious to the refugees streaming down the street. Everyone solemnly weighs the enormity of his words.

Wolfgang looks and asks, "The same Heinz Guderian who pioneered the cruel strategy behind German's armored warfare?"

The ambassador nods, his pallor ashen with grief. "You must go before the collapse of the citadel at Brest. Time is short. I fear it will only take a few days for Guderian to complete his stranglehold on the city. When he does, it will be too late for any of us to escape."

Ferdek takes the letter and places it in the vest pocket of his jacket. He solemnly asks, "What about you, Father?"

Trying to exude confidence to the young, he remarks, "I have plans. I will do what is best for Poland. Now, take our treasured copy and learn what it has to teach. If you can do that, then we can start altering the future of these invaders. I suggest you head for Romania, then go due west through Hungary to bypass the new German territories. Your travel should take you to Switzerland. You will find refuge there in your family's chalet, Wolfgang."

Ferdek, Tavius, and Wolfgang grudgingly accept the petition. Ferdek confirms, "My sister and I will take the letter to the airport to catch the plane before it departs. You two, round up your families. We'll meet up at the Barbican Gate no later than six o'clock."

Wolfgang warns, "It may take us longer than that."

Ferdek counters, "Time is ticking and not in our favor. The longer we wait, the more time will pass before we deliver Baby to the allies. Every second we lose, someone else dies. We must move now and quickly."

Ferdek grabs Patricia's hand and briskly pulls her away from the royal castle. But she plants her feet and turns. "Papa, you are coming, too, aren't you?"

The ambassador smiles sadly. "Scamper, my children. I have two vehicles waiting for you in the courtyard. There should be enough fuel in them for you to reach your destination. Godspeed. Our country depends on you."

Ferdek, Tavius, and Wolfgang run toward the courtyard. Ferdek drags Patrycja by the hand as she keeps looking back at her father. She lets her tears fall after he disappears in a horde of Polish people frantically pushing their way out of town.

Chapter 17

At Warsaw Chopin Airport, a lone plane sits on the runway with a line of Polish diplomats making their way up the stairs. It appears the loading will complete before sunset.

Ferdek wheels past the gate and pulls to a stop behind the plane. He gets out and hurries to the bottom of the stairs. Ferdek abruptly halts face-to-face with an aging diplomat, who smiles with recognition.

"Ferdek, my boy, are you leaving with us?"

"No, sir. I have a message for Phillip Kandinsky. It's from my father."

"Is your father coming with us?"

"The message is urgent. Is Phillip Kandinsky here?"

The diplomat steps back and motions Ferdek forward. "Then go, please. I certainly don't want the flight delayed any longer than necessary."

Ferdek nods his thanks and races up the stairs. Inside the airplane, he looks across the faces of the passengers and loudly proclaims, "I have a message for Mister Phillip Kandinsky... Phillip Kandinsky."

A gentleman stands beside the seat on the third row, dressed well and distinguished. I'm Phillip Kandinsky. Is there something wrong?"

Ferdek removes the envelope from his jacket pocket and hands it to the man. "I was asked to give you this. You must deliver it to President Sikorski as quickly as possible."

Kandinsky bristles and indignantly states, "I am afraid you have made a grave mistake, young man. Wladyslaw Sikorski is not the president of Poland."

Other passengers cease stowing bags and fall silent, waiting for the response.

"He may be by the time you arrive," Ferdek replies.

Kandinsky frowns with confusion. "Who is sending me this letter?"

Ferdek offers, "My father."

"And who is your father?"

Ferdek states, "Ambassador Ferdek Watcowski."

Kandinsky slips the letter into his coat pocket. "Is this a record of Poland's past?"

Ferdek smiles with confidence. "No, sir. It is the blueprint for Poland's future."

Ferdek deplanes. He watches the aircraft take off, staring until it ascends beyond the clouds. Ferdek turns and runs to the car and climbs behind the wheel, revs up the motor, and spins around, heading for the gate with great haste. "It's done."

"I pray that the letter reaches the new president." Patrycja sighs.

"I pray that the new president is still alive when the letter arrives."

"You fear for his life?"

"I fear for Poland."

Ferdek accelerates and speeds through the gate. He heads toward the highway, determined to make their rendezvous with the others on time. However, in the late afternoon, the Warsaw traffic is at a virtual standstill. Cars jammed bumper-to-bumper as they inch their way out of town. Horns are honking. Ferdek slumps over the steering wheel. Beads of sweat roll down his face. "We are running late."

Patrycja looks ahead for openings to escape the snail's pace. "There's nothing you can do about it."

"I told Tavius and Wolfgang to have their families ready to leave by six. It's already a few minutes shy of seven."

"If you're late because of this traffic, it stands to reason that they will be late as well."

Ferdek slaps the steering wheel. "Wasting time is the deadliest sin I can think of committing. Time is against us."

"Time runs at its speed. We can't slow it down or stop it. We have to make do with the time that is given us."

"You may be a poet, Patrycja, but you're certainly not a soldier."

It is nearly eight when Ferdek steers the car off the highway and is captured in the traffic headed toward the Barbican Gate. He parks the car and eases outside, looking around. Cars are entangled and at a near standstill down the street. He searches for Tavius, Wolfgang, and the families, but there is no sign of them.

Ferdek walks around to the front of the car and climbs onto the hood. He sits, head in his hands, and waits. Patrycja climbs up alongside him and surveys the crowded streets with a concerned look on her face.

Ferdek growls, "They're late."

"The traffic is terrible. Wait. They wouldn't leave without us."

Ferdek tenses as cannon fire and exploding shells echo in bursts of color to light up the horizon.

Ferdek moans, "The Germans are coming closer. They are already at the back gates of the town, and we have no one to stop them. We must leave and leave now."

"Tavius and Wolfgang would not leave you. We wait."

Ferdek glances up at the watchtower. "Five more minutes, and then we go."

"Ten."

01010101001100

Tavius' stomach knots as he drives with his jaws clenched through the pressing horde of cars, trucks, and people progressing down the road. The street is bombarded by horns honking and people shouting. He pulls to a stop and turns around to get his bearings. His face brightens as he sees Patrycja standing on the hood of Ferdek's car by the Barbican Gate, her hand shielding her face as if she searches for some sign of him.

Tavius waves to get her attention and calms as soon as she raises both hands in acknowledgment. Tavius fights his way through the traffic to Ferdek's car.

"I expected you here two hours ago."

Looking through the windshield, Tavius confesses, "I had an unexpected problem."

Ferdek notices that it is only Tavius. "Where's your family? You went to get them. Are they coming? How much longer will they take? We had orders to take our families out of Warsaw as soon as possible."

A shadow of grief passes over Tavius's face as he steps out of the vehicle. "That's the problem. My father had a stroke late last evening. He's in the hospital, and my mother says she will not leave without him."

Patrycja places a gentle and comforting hand on his shoulder. "Tavius, I am so sorry. How bad is it? What are the doctors telling you?"

"Nothing. The doctors are telling us absolutely nothing. Wounded soldiers and civilians pack the hospital crowding the halls, and there are no rooms left. The doctors haven't even seen my father yet. He lies on a cot in the morgue while my mother cries over him. The hospital is full of mothers crying. Who knows if my father will even still be alive when a doctor comes to treat him. He is already in a coma and may never open his eyes again."

"How is your mother dealing with this?"

"Feisty as always. As soon as Mother saw the chaos in the hospital, she grabbed a nurse's dress from the supply cabinet and tried to comfort those who are in as much distress as she is. Mother knows the end is near for both father and Warsaw. I pleaded with her to come with me, but she begged me to go. She does not know the mission we are on, but she knows it must be important. She insisted for Poland to survive, we must prevail. She will pray for every step we take while we are gone."

Ferdek claps his friend on the back. "She is a brave woman."

Tavius nods. "Mother insists on doing what's right. She is Polish after all."

Chapter 18

The setting sun is shrouding the downtown street in shadows of darkness as Wolfgang places a heavy suitcase against the wall of a building. He helps his father, Kondrat, sit down on it. The older man appears dejected as he leans his head against the wall. Wolfgang pats his shoulder to reassure him. "I won't be gone long, Father. Just take a breather and wait until I get back. We have a lot of miles ahead of us."

Kondrat clutches at his son's coat, frightened. "What if you don't come back?"

"Trust me, Father. I'll be back before you know I'm gone."

"Wolfgang?"

"Yes, Father?"

"Promise me one thing."

"What is it?"

"When the time comes, and I fear it's not too far distant, I want you to bury me in Polish soil."

Wolfgang pats his father's shoulder again. "We still have a lot of living to do. When we are tired, we worry about things that usually never happen."

"Promise me, Wolfgang."

"I will, Father. If anything happens to you, and I pray that it doesn't, I will bring you home.

Kondrat closes his eyes wearing a sad but satisfied smile.

Wolfgang moves purposefully down the street until he finds the side street to his destination. He quickly turns into it and searches the delivery door of a small church. He turns the knob and steps inside. Wolfgang ventures into the dark sanctuary. Only the spotty rays of a dreary moon cut their way through the darkness. Wolfgang hurries toward the pews. Father Nowak, a young priest, nervously awaits him.

Wolfgang sits. Father Nowak pulls a prominent roll of paper out of his robe. "I have the information you requested, Wolfgang."

Wolfgang accepts the paper with a grateful smile. "I am forever indebted to you, Father Nowak."

"No, Wolfgang, you are indebted to Ludek and especially Rysiek. Two boys really, trying to be men, wanting to be soldiers. They were able to map those areas where the Germans are digging their trenches. Ludek managed to return with the map. Rysiek did not."

Wolfgang frowns with concern. "Has he been hurt? Captured?"

"A bullet in his throat. Ludek was hit, too, in the shoulder. He managed to reach the church. You will find the map stained with Rysiek's blood. He was a brave young man."

"I'm sorry, Father Nowak. I will say prayers for them and their families."

"We live. We die. It is not ours to question when or why. It is destiny. That's all. I pray that you succeed, Wolfgang. All of Poland prays for you. They don't know it, but I know they do. Now be gone with you."

Father Nowak rises, and the two men shake hands. Wolfgang starts to say something, then thinks better of it. Father Nowak turns away to the front of the church. Wolfgang heads to the exits as Father Nowak steps through the empty pews and looks at the stained-glass window high above the street. Illumination from the bright moon shines through a break in the clouds. The cross in the window reflects colored prisms on the floor.

Wolfgang locates his father. Kondrat brightens somewhat with their departure. Wolfgang holds tightly to his father's arm while pushing against the crowds shoving their way in the opposite direction. Both carry heavy suitcases, struggling to negotiate the cobblestones. Kondrat stares down, a portrait of sadness.

Wolfgang and Kondrat reach the roadsters, and immediately Ferdek senses a problem. "Everything well, Wolfgang?"

Wolfgang tries to remain positive. "We're good. It's just that we had a little trouble, uh, packing."

Tavius rushes to take Kondrat's suitcase. Kondrat turns and sits on the running board of the car, gasping for air.

Wolfgang plays the part of the peacemaker with a forced grin. "You know how some people are about their keepsakes and pictures. You should have seen the suitcases we left behind."

"If we get out of Poland alive, we can buy other suitcases."

Wolfgang, losing his bravado, says, "It's not the suitcases. It's about their keepsakes and pictures."

Ferdek observes, "It's difficult to pack seventy years into a single suitcase. Our parents are leaving with everything they had when they came into the world."

Tavius purses his lips sadly. "Nothing."

Wolfgang clears his throat after a silent headcount. "We seem to be a little short of some passengers. Tavius, I thought your parents were coming with you."

Tavius turns and stares down the crowded street. "I'll be going alone."

Wolfgang starts to say something but Ferdek locks eyes with him and shakes his head. Wolfgang looks up at a darkening sky. "Ferdek, it's getting late. How long before the ambassador and your mother arrive?"

Patrycja draws a ragged breath but remains stoically silent.

Ferdek senses her turmoil and acknowledges, "No one else is coming. Mother and Father indicated they would leave with the rest of the diplomatic party. It's just the five of us.

Tavius adds, "And Baby."

Wolfgang jumps into a car and states, "Let me lead us out. I know the backroads around here quite well. I received all the last known troop movements from a contact of mine on the way here. It will be dark soon, and I am confident we can slip out without drawing too much attention."

Tavius cynically comments, "All the other refugees are probably saying the same thing."

Wolfgang nods. "But we have to try."

Ferdek challenges, "No. We have to succeed. If only one survives, he, or she, must make sure that Baby gets to the allies." Ferdek looks at Patrycja.

Patrycja looks surprised and stammers, "I don't even know what Baby is."

"You'll know in time, little sister."

Patrycja says, "You mentioned it was an ultimate weapon. Will it go boom if I hold it the wrong way?"

"It's not a bomb.

"That's good to know."

"Ferdek, in case I have to rescue Baby, where is she hidden?"

"I'll show you later tonight."

"What if we don't last that long?

Ferdek sighs. "Then we are doomed, my little sister.

"The whole world as we know it is doomed," Tavius laments, "and Poland will be nothing more than a sand pebble at the bottom of a bomb blast.

Patrycja shudders. "That's not a very pretty picture, Tavius. I believe we will succeed."

Tavius shrugs. "It's not a very pretty war."

Ferdek watches the horde of refugees fight their way toward the edge of town. A few cars ease through the crowd. Most are fleeing Warsaw on foot.

Ferdek gets into the other roadster. "Everyone, take a seat. Darkness will be upon us within the hour. We'll travel at night and rest during the day.

Wolfgang agrees, "It's safer that way."

Chapter 19

For Ferdek, Wolfgang, Tavius, Patrycja, and Kondrat it is a discouraging scene. Even though it is nighttime in the countryside, the Polish military is in full retreat. The refugees can see the soldiers' weariness from their roadsters. Soldiers carry the wounded out of the woodlands on stretchers, and soldiers are dropping, unable to go any farther. Ferdek sees Polish troops strung out, but it's too dark to see how far in the distance. The soldiers crawl and collapse as bombs dropping on the horizon send up deadly flares, and the ground shakes from the force of the explosions.

An officer's car races down the road, weaving through the crowd of refugees in search of safety. As the traffic stalls, the five watch guiltily as that car stops beside a Polish sergeant kneeling by the side of the road.

A Polish captain leaps from the car and angrily grabs the sergeant's arm, yanking him to his feet, and screams, "What's going on here, Sergeant? Your mission was to protect Warsaw, but here I find you and your army in total disarray."

The weary sergeant climbs unsteadily to his feet and salutes. "We can fight no more, sir."

Astonished, the Polish captain demands, "What do you mean you can't fight. You're a soldier. You have a job to do. We're at war."

The sergeant sadly proclaims, "The war in Poland is over."

The captain disgustedly roars, "Where is your commanding officer?"

The sergeant wistfully states, "He's dead, sir."

"Then the second in command?"

"He died in the first wave. They're all dead, sir. Our military is in shreds."

The captain, growing fearful, asks, "Who's in command now?"

"We have no command, sir. We only have the dead and the dying."

"Where are you and your men going?"

"Romania if we live long enough to reach the border.

"You may as well turn around and fight, Sergeant. The Germans will hunt you down like little foxes in Romania."

"By the time the Germans get there, sir, we'll be gone."

"You can't run! There is no room for cowards in our army. It is time to stand strong and fight for your country."

"If you must fight, sir, then you must fight but look around you. When the fight reaches you, you'll be standing in the middle of this road alone." The sergeant trudges away. He holds his head down, utterly indifferent to the fuming captain.

"Sergeant, you can't walk away from me while I'm talking to you. It is forbidden. You will face a military court-martial and execution for desertion."

But the sergeant keeps walking until he disappears in the darkness.

The traffic clears. Wolfgang and Tavius drive the two roadsters with their passengers down the road and into the darkness. No one says anything about the sobering drama they all witnessed.

Chapter 20

The faint blush on the horizon announces it is almost sunrise. Ferdek jerks his car off the roadway and jumps out as soon as it rolls to a stop. Patrycja climbs from her seat and runs around the front of the vehicle. He surveys the perimeter, verifying they are mostly hidden.

Ferdek motions, and Tavius pulls his car in behind them under the last branch. Their faces mirror the terror they feel from the sight slowly unfolding before them. In the growing light, they all see the extent of the retreat. An army of stragglers moves across the fields, heading southeast toward Romania. Soldiers in the first wave are taking their tracked vehicles with them.

The retreating army shadowy figures in the dust kicked up by the vehicles negotiating surfaces chopped up by bombs, tanks, and heavy artillery.

Ferdek cringes against the ground that's shaking from the explosions. The impending drone of approaching fighter airplanes.

Patrycja asks, "What's happening?"

"That's what's left of our army," Ferdek grimly replies. "They no longer have the will to fight. It's a war they know they can't win. We lost before the first shot."

Tavius repositions his vehicle alongside the first. Ferdek points toward a small outcropping of trees. "We need to reach that cover now. The Stukageschwaders will be out prowling for anything with an ounce of life. Soldiers, civilians, or refugees, it won't matter to them."

The sound of the incoming siren scream announces a Stukageschwader banking out of the sky. Ferdek grabs his sister's hand, pulling her behind him as the fighter's nose is headed straight toward them. "Too LATE."

The Stuka is clearly on a strafing run, sending several 7.92 mm rounds toward each vehicle that hits on the road ahead of them. The plane passes overhead and swings around for another run.

Ferdek and Patrycja scramble into the roadster and race the engine driving zigzags behind the matching roadster. Both vehicles bounce toward the trees. The Stuka is intent on killing as the guns fire. Bullets rip up the ground as rancid gunpowder smells fill the air of the rising dust. Several shots tear into Ferdek's car, and it spins in and out of control with his driving skill at its limits. The radiator explodes. Both vehicles limp into the tree line border of the forest, tires flat. Smoke pours from beneath the hood of Ferdek's car.

Ferdek rolls out of the car. Patrycja falls out of the roadster, regains her balance, and runs toward Tavius. He takes her hand, and they run further into the thicker woods. Ferdek is only a few steps behind. Wolfgang hustles his father out of the car driven by Tavius, but they can't run nearly as fast.

The Stuka circles once more. It dives out of the sun rising above the trees—the ground beside Wolfgang and Kondrat tears apart by the bullets. Clumps of grass ricochet off them as they hurry toward hopeful safety. Wolfgang and Kondrat fall beneath splintered tree limbs and a cloud of dust that encircles them. Ferdek, Tavius, and Patrycja look back over their shoulders, their faces tense, fearing they have lost Wolfgang and his father. Patrycja spins and sprints toward them.

As the dust settles, Wolfgang and Kondrat slowly open their eyes. They are staring at each other, then choking on smoke and dust. Kondrat suddenly laughs. Wolfgang laughs even louder as Patrycja kneels beside them.

"Are you alright?"

Wolfgang howls to his father. "I told you they couldn't kill us."

Kondrat tries to catch his breath. "Forget what I told you."

"What did you tell me?"

"That I wanted you to bring me back home and bury me in good Polish dirt when I die."

"Why should I forget it?"

Kondrat laughs harder. "I've changed my mind. I'm not dying."

The sound of the Stuka fades into the distance, and the forest is once again quiet. Wolfgang stands and helps his father to his feet. Patrycja gently wipes the dust from the older man's face.

Wolfgang looks toward the roadsters. "We need to assess the damage to the cars. We have to stay mobile, and those vehicles are our only ticket to Switzerland."

Patrycja says, "The Stuka hit both vehicles pretty hard. We have flat tires and shot-up motors. One radiator burned, and multiple bullet holes in the sides. I doubt if those cars can make it out of the forest. They surely don't stand a chance of reaching Switzerland."

Tavius disagrees, "I don't know, Patrycja. I'm something of an automobile tinkerer. Heck, I've done work on racing machines in competition. I might be able to get them up and running if I had the tools."

"My father always kept a fairly complete set of tools in the trunk. He once was a pretty fair tinkerer on automobiles, too. He went out alone in the garage on worked on cars when he wanted to escape the stress of his job. He could take a pipe and an old driveshaft and turn them into a workable machine gun. Maybe he knew the war was coming before the rest of us did." Ferdek strides through the trees and back toward the wounded vehicles.

The car repairs continued in full swing throughout the day as evening blanketed the forest.

Patrycja sits with her back to a tree. She has a piece of paper in her lap and holds a pen in her hand.

Ferdek slumps down beside her. "What are you doing?"

"Writing a letter."

"Who's the lucky guy?"

"Father."

"Why bother? You'll see him in a few days. We'll make Switzerland in a couple of days, and father is on his way with the diplomatic corps. By the weekend, we'll all be sitting down to dinner in the embassy."

"Then again, we may not make it. Perhaps the diplomatic corps never left Warsaw. If the Germans get there first, they'll shut down the airport. Father will be stranded, and some German official will want to try him for war crimes."

"Father's not a criminal, Patrycja."

"He is the way Germans think. If you're not one of them, you are a criminal. It's prison or death, and one is about as bad as the other."

"I'm betting Father makes it out of Poland just fine."

"I'd say his chances are much better than ours."

Ferdek stares at his sister, who returns the gaze. "If I don't reach Switzerland, maybe my letter will."

Ferdek touches her shoulder, then stands without a word. He makes his way back into the forest to their makeshift repair shop.

Tavius has labored for hours on the engine of the roadster. He raises up releasing some of the kinks. Ferdek grimly nods while Tavius wipes his hands on a rag as Ferdek walks toward him.

Ferdek asks, "How bad is it?"

"We have three flats and one shot-up radiator that will never work right again."

"So, what options do we have?"

"I can't salvage both vehicles, but we can take the right parts from the car that's suffered the most damage and make one vehicle whole again."

Ferdek brightens and nods. "Let's do it."

"It was excellent planning on your father's part. We are indeed fortunate he secured the same make and model of roadsters."

"When do you think you will have a car up and running, Tavius?"

"I believe we planned to travel by dark and rest by day."

"That's what we decided."

"Then plan on leaving sometime after dark."

"You're a magician, Tavius."

"Just a wunderkind with a wrench." Tavius turns and shouts, "Wolfgang, give me a hand and let's see how well we can transplant the parts and convince them to start working together."

Wolfgang removes the nuts from the one good tire on Ferdek's car.

"I'll start on the logistics and let Patrycja and Kondrat know when we expect to leave. Then I'll consolidate our supplies, so we'll be packed and ready to load as soon as you give us the word, gentlemen."

Patrycja helps Kondrat drink some water from a cup while he rests against the trunk of a tree. Ferdek approaches. "How is he?"

Patrycja smiles. "He's a little rattled from the ordeal, but Kondrat is a real trooper." The man smiles at her words. They are reassuring, but Patrycja's eyes tell Ferdek of her concern for his well-being.

"We were lucky the cars took the bullets, rather than any of us."

Kondrat asks, "How long do you think we will be here?"

"Tavius assures me we'll be going soon after dark. We'll only have one car. It will be a little crowded."

Kondrat uneasily asks, "Will it outrun the Germans?"

"It has so far."

At sundown, Ferdek adjusts his backpack and finishes loading supplies in the trunk of the roadster. The consolidation effort of two roadsters into one is complete.

Tavius drops wearily beside the back tire. Wolfgang sags to the ground beside him.

Tavius announces, "We have an operational vehicle. It's ready to go, but I'm not sure Wolfgang and I are. We're exhausted."

Wolfgang petitions, "Do you think we can spare a few hours of sleep before we hit the roads that take us to Switzerland?"

"We can't leave until dark anyway. A little sleep and a bite to eat would do us all good."

"Right now, I'd rather sleep, Ferdek. We can eat in the car. It'll be cold anyway. No sense in a fire burning out here as it would draw the Germans like moths. Nobody is supposed to be here."

Patrycja hurries into the clearing, leading Kondrat by the hand. Her face is panicked as if she saw some horror. "Forget any sleep."

Tavius is on his feet. "What's wrong?"

Patrycja points toward the outer edge of the forest.

A tank platoon is churning its way across an open field toward them. One lone spotlight scans the ground in a 180° semi-circle. Ferdek is on one knee looking over the hood of the roadster. "We've got a platoon of inbound tanks and infantry heading straight for us. Everything's loaded. We've got to make a run for it if they don't change direction."

Patrycja queries, "What can stop them?"

Wolfgang speculates, "They may not want to fight their way through the trees."

Ferdek orders, "Everybody down." Everyone lies belly flat on the ground, watching the approaching tanks with bated breath.

Patrycja pleads, "I wish the sun were down."

Tavius notes, "Why?"

"These old roadsters cast off a pretty good reflection when the sun hits them just right."

Wolfgang urges, "Just pray the shadows reach us before the sun does."

Kondrat suggests, "If you're not prayed up by now, it's too late to start."

Ferdek, Tavius, Wolfgang, Patrycja, and Kondrat watch the tank column move closer to the forest. It is almost upon them but has yet to discover the refugees.

Ferdek states, "We have a decision to make."

Patrycja asks, "Now?"

"Time's not in our favor."

Then, without warning, a hundred yards from the forest, the tank column suddenly turns. The field artillery and foot soldiers follow it. Five pairs of eyes focus on the German iron cross emblazoned on the tanks.

Wolfgang remarks, "That's the most frightening sight of all."

Patrycja cringes. "Makes my blood run cold."

Tavius derisively glares at the passing war machines. "I wonder how much Polish blood it has spilled today."

Ferdek wipes his brow with his soiled handkerchief. "A single drop was a drop too much."

The vehicles disappear over a slight rise. Wolfgang stands and paces back and forth in front of the roadster as the last glow of daylight fades. "I'm not for sure I understand what's going on. We are heading southeast, but the tank column is moving west. Why? It doesn't make any sense. What's more, it doesn't look like they are moving to engage our army. It appears more like they are on maneuvers, on their way back into Poland."

Tavius suggests, "Perhaps the fight is over, and they are being called back to the capital."

Ferdek challenges, "If the fight is over, then why aren't they out mopping up the last pockets of resistance? From what we saw earlier, all surviving forces of the Polish army are going southeast, which must mean they are retreating to Romania. So, the Germans should be moving southeast as well. You're right, Wolfgang. It just doesn't make any sense."

"I don't know about the rest of you, but after this little encounter, I'm not sleepy at all. I'd just as soon sneak out of here when the troops are out of sight."

Patrycja arrives at Wolfgang's side. She gently tugs his arm, leading him to where his father has been sleeping. Tears roll down Patrycja's cheeks. Wolfgang looks down at his father, and tears gather in his eyes, as well. He takes a deep breath.

Wolfgang announces, "September seventeenth." After a painful sigh, he adds, "Happy birthday, Father."

"You should be proud of him, Wolfgang. He gave his last breath for the Poland he loved."

"His last wish was to be buried in the ground of his homeland."

Ferdek places a brotherly arm around Wolfgang's shoulders. "And so he shall be."

Tavius suggests, "I did find a small trenching shovel among the tools. I would esteem it an honor to help bury Kondrat."

Wolfgang draws a ragged breath and nods. Tavius walks to the trunk of the car, opens it, and withdraws the small trenching tool. He and Wolfgang find a spot of soft dirt among the trees and break into the earth.

Ferdek draws a pair of field glass binoculars from beneath the front seat and walks to the forest's edge. He pans the twilight horizon. Patrycja follows a step behind.

Ferdek comments, "The Germans are moving off to the west at a leisurely pace. That troubles me."

"Why?"

"It just doesn't add up. What are they looking for?"

"Maybe they're looking for us."

Ferdek lets the binoculars hang down around his neck. His mind races with thoughts. "We're wasting too much time. We need to leave, and we need to leave this instant." He looks at Patrycja for agreement, but her glare is worse than a slap across the face.

"Maybe we should, but we won't."

"He's just an old man. His time had come."

"He's not just an old man. He's Wolfgang's father."

"Wolfgang knows how important our mission is."

"Let me ask you one question then."

"What?"

"If that was our father, would you have just walked off and left him lying on the ground without giving him a Christian burial?"

"He would have been a casualty of war." Ferdek reflected for a few seconds. "But, no, I wouldn't have left him."

The small trenching tool simply does not remove soil as fast as they want. But finally, the men reach the needed depth for Kondrat's final resting place. Wolfgang hammers the last clod of dirt into the mound of his father's grave then looks up at everyone.

"My deepest thanks to all of you. I know it was ill-advised to spend the time it took to dig a grave, but I could not have lived with myself if I hadn't."

Ferdek reaches down, grasps Wolfgang's hand, and helps him to his feet. "It was only proper that you bury your father. No apologies. He died among friends, and he died a free man. I only hope we, too, will enjoy a full ending to our stories."

Tavius suggests, "May I recommend that you mark this location with stones so at some point you can retrieve his remains for a proper burial?"

Wolfgang eyes everyone for their permission. After their silent agreement, he hurries farther into the woodlands. Patrycja and Tavius collect rocks. Only Ferdek is left alone to stew at another waste of time. Finally, he picks up rocks as well.

Patrycja whispers to Ferdek, "I knew you had a heart."

"I just thought it would go faster if I pitched in to help."

Patrycja shows a satisfied smile as she winks at Ferdek.

Chapter 21

Wolfgang says prayers as they pay their final respects. Each person collects the tools they used. They return them to the boot of the roaster and resume the journey once again. Now in darkness, the roadster eases slowly across the empty landscape, the road dimly illuminated by the dirty headlights and the glow of a half-moon hanging crooked in the sky.

Wolfgang is behind the wheel, and Ferdek is in the passenger's seat. Tavius and Patrycja are in the backseat. Each is alone with their thoughts.

Wolfgang admits, "I may not be going as fast as you want, Ferdek, but I need to go slow so we can watch for any possible troop movement or make sure we don't hit a deer. We have often hunted in this area, which is why I know the land around here."

"Any idea where we are exactly? We should be getting fairly close to Brest Litovsk. Father said our army is defending the town, but he was afraid it would soon be surrounded and under siege."

Tavius adds his perspective. "If our army is still in control, we can find partisans who will be able to smuggle us into Switzerland. It would be a lot safer than roaring across the country and trying to stay hidden while driving a fancy roadster."

"That may be wishful thinking on your part, Tavius," Wolfgang cautions. "I think we should head straight to the Romanian border just as the remnants of our army did. They may be as dangerous as the Germans. It doesn't take long before a rogue army becomes a band of outlaws. Survival of the fittest is the way I've heard it explained."

Ferdek suggests, "I think we should at least find out what the situation is in Brest Litovsk. I may be wrong; then again, I may be right. I believe we owe it to ourselves to take a quick look. Just running without knowing if our army broke the German siege seems wrong.

"It's a fool's errand, Ferdek," Wolfgang states.

"Possibly. But we have a few hours before daylight. Tavius and I can sneak in close, take a quick look, assess the situation, and be back in a couple of hours."

"What if you're not back in two hours?"

"I'm leaving Baby with you. You know the mission, and you know what's at stake. I trust you completely. If we are not back in two hours, chances are we're not coming back, so don't wait."

Patrycja anxiously chirps, "Don't I get a vote? I think you may be walking into a death trap. I think we should bypass Brest Litovsk as though it never existed."

Ferdek says, "You are keeping Baby. That is much more important than a vote."

"I don't even know what Baby is."

"Tavius, Wolfgang, and I are just soldiers who are fighting for a cause dear to us. In the overall scheme of our existence, it matters little if we live or if we die. But, Baby? Baby can win the war."

Chapter 22

A few kilometers away, in a lonely farmhouse, General Eberhardt sits at a wooden table across from Henningsen. The house is cloaked in darkness and melts into the shadows with a single flickering light periodically visible from the only window. Inside, the room offers a single kerosene lantern. The general fidgets with annoyance visible on his face and his lips a straight line of displeasure at the situation.

General Eberhardt rants, "I am extremely disappointed, Lieutenant. You had one mission to accomplish, and you have failed the Fuhrer miserably."

"We have only been searching for two days, sir."

"There are only three of them."

"It's a big country."

Eberhardt slams his fist on the table. "No, Lieutenant. Poland is a small country, and we control it from border to border. Its pathetic army is in full retreat, and the country is in total disarray. I have given you all of the men you requested, and you have given me nothing."

"The roads are packed with refugees. It is difficult to get from one town to another. Towns are burning. The men we seek could be anywhere."

"They could be right under your nose, Lieutenant." He shook off the comment. "I don't care where they are. I want you to find them. I want you to arrest them. Kill them if you have to, but they must not reach the border."

"Which border?"

Eberhardt rises to his full height and shrieks, "Any of them. All of them. You know what they have stolen from us."

"I do, sir."

Eberhardt sits again. "It must not reach the allies. It must not leave Poland. If it does, Lieutenant, may God have mercy on you. The Fuhrer will have a firing squad waiting for you."

Henningsen stands at attention. "I can assure you, sir, that my men will cover all exits from Poland. We will leave early morning."

"No, Lieutenant, you and your men will leave tonight."

The general rests his elbows on the table, his face in his hands, as he hears the lieutenant's footsteps cross the floor. The lieutenant slams the door as he leaves.

Chapter 23

Blanketed in darkness, Ferdek and Tavius slip toward a sleeping city of Brest Litovsk. They find the perimeter of the town teeming with soldiers, tanks, and heavy artillery.

In low tones, Tavius remarks, "It looks like a city under siege."

"I think it looks more like a city that was surrounded and captured. The people inside might as well be in prison. None are getting out." He adds after a pause, "None are getting out alive."

"Another city we have lost."

"We have lost the whole country."

"The Germans have taken our land, and now they are squeezing the life out of our people."

Ferdek kneels and uses his binoculars. He methodically scans the dark city, lit only by the headlights of trucks moving in and out of the town. A vehicle passes in front of the lens. An iron cross does not mark it, but instead, it bears the hammer and sickle of the Soviets.

Ferdek sucks in his breath. "It's not the Germans."

"What do you mean?"

Ferdek passes the binoculars to Tavius. "The Russians now have control of Brest Litovsk. We are at their mercy, Tavius."

"I thought the Russians were our allies."

"My father did everything he could for an alliance with Russia, but it seems it decided to make a deal with the devil. Russia made a deal with Hitler himself. Split up Poland and divide the spoils. Our army never had a chance. Our soldiers were dead before they ever went into battle."

Still scanning the area, Tavius spots a gypsy wagon sitting beside a crumbling wall. Mizella is on his knees, waving frantically. Halina is being dragged away by two Russian soldiers.

Tavius hands the binoculars back to Ferdek. "Hurry. Look to the right at about two o'clock. The gate leading into the old town. We have some friends in trouble."

Ferdek grabs the binoculars and swings in the indicated direction. A Russian soldier slams the butt of his rifle hard against Mizella's head, and the gypsy leader collapses to the ground. He tries to stand, but the soldier kicks him in the stomach. The soldier laughs as his comrades trying to quell an angry Halina, fighting desperately to wrest herself free from their grasp. Her frantic efforts entertain the Russian soldiers.

"Tavius, we can't just leave her."

"We have no choice."

"We always have a choice."

"But our mission is much more important than a girl's life."

"Tell that to Halina. She saved us once. Without her, our mission would have already failed. We can't let her die." He adds, "Or worse."

"We'll never make it back in time."

"We won't take long. The difference between living and dying is never longer than the snap of a finger."

Ferdek rises and runs toward the old town gate as he calls over his shoulder. "You coming?"

Tavius sighs and quickly follows his friend.

Chapter 24

Hidden among a cluster of trees surrounded by the darkness, an agitated Wolfgang frets in the seat of the roadster. He checks his watch yet again. "It's been more than two hours."

Patrycja stares out the open window beside her, a worried frown on her face. "Give them another ten minutes."

"We've already given them thirty."

"They're coming back. I know they are. I feel it right down here in the pit of my stomach. We need to wait a little longer. We can't abandon our family and friends."

"I know what you're going through, Patrycja. My nerves are on edge, too. But we had a plan. It was Ferdek's plan, and he's counting on us. We can't let Poland down." Wolfgang reluctantly starts the car engine.

Patrycja sticks her head out the window and yells, "Ferdek. Ferdek. Tavius. Where are you?" It is a failed wail into the empty night.

"They can't hear you."

"I know they're not dead."

"Then we'll see them somewhere near the border on the road to Cernauti."

Patrycja cries softly, her face in her hands, as Wolfgang drives into the night.

Chapter 25

Ferdek rushes toward Mizella who lies groaning on the ground. He observes as Mizella flinches at the noise, then covers his face with both arms, likely expecting a soldier to kick him again.

Ferdek kneels beside Mizella and gently asks, "What happened? What's going on?" Carefully, Ferdek helps the gypsy to a sitting position.

"They have Halina!"

"We know."

"The Russians are dogs."

Tavius declares, "We'll get her back, Mizella."

"How?"

"Tell him, Ferdek."

"We'll figure it out." Ferdek looks around at the darkness. The soldiers are gone. "How quick can you have the wagon ready to leave?"

"She's ready now."

"Horses fresh?"

"They haven't run all day."

"Be on the seat and ready to go when we get back."

"How long will that be?"

"Maybe five minutes. Maybe never. But be ready to leave because we'll be running for our lives." After a quick pause, Ferdek asks, "Do you have a pistol?"

Mizella grins. "Only one."

Ferdek advances, "One is enough."

Mizella reaches behind the seat of a wagon and withdraws an old pistol. He hands it to Ferdek. "It's loaded."

Ferdek shoves the pistol in his belt and walks toward the gate; Tavius is close behind. Once through the gate, Ferdek and Tavius ease down the street. There are several tiny houses but no lights. All is silent.

A woman screams in the house on the corner. There is a single light on in an upstairs room. Ferdek jerks his head toward the scream and darts across the street, keeping to the shadows. He runs onto the porch and tries the door, but it is locked. Ferdek looks at Tavius, takes a long breath, and kicks in the door. They burst inside, but the room is empty.

Taking the stairs, Ferdek reaches the first landing just as a Russian soldier appears at the top of the stairs. He's barefoot, missing a shirt, and his belt is unbuckled. The soldier doesn't say a word—the first bullet drills into his forehead. He grabs the dead solder and drags him down the hallway; Tavius is right behind him. Ferdek reaches the open door of the lit room, pauses a moment, and then throws the dead soldier inside. Bullets riddle the body.

Ferdek rolls toward the open door where a Russian soldier stands in his underwear staring at the fallen body of his comrade. He is in a stupor the liquor buzz long gone. In one motion, Ferdek rises to his feet and jams the muzzle of his pistol against the soldier's head as Tavius jerks the gun from his hand. The soldier looks as if he can't quite comprehend what is going on.

Halina is off the bed and on her feet grasping a torn and tattered dress around her naked body.

"You alright?"

Halina doesn't answer. Her face flushed with anger.

Tavius nods toward the Russian soldier. "What do we do with him?"

"You will do nothing with him." Halina rips the pistol from Ferdek's grasp, shoves the muzzle between the soldier's eyes, and pulls the trigger. The soldier's head jerks back and blood splatters on her face. She doesn't blink.

Tavius asks, "Now what?"

"Now we run like hell, Tavius, and hope we're out of sight before somebody finds them."

Halina finishes putting on her dress. Blood stains her face, and anger flashes in her eyes. No regrets. Ferdek takes her hand, and the three of them run out of the room and bolt down the stairs. They head straight for the gate.

Chapter 26

Mizella pushes the horses hard all night. As the sun peers just over the horizon, the gypsy wagon races out of the forest. It travels across the remains of a battlefield toward the road leading to the border between Poland and Romania.

The traffic is jammed nearly to a stop with vehicles and refugees fleeing the German occupation. The wagon rolls at a steady pace parallel to the other escapees. Mizella slows the horses. He is content with Halina right by his side. Ferdek kneels in the open door behind them.

Halina chortles. "We are making better time than any of them."

Mizella laughs too. "The horses don't need a road. We make our road and go where we please, and maybe

Romania will treat us better than the Germans or the Russians did."

Ferdek questions, "How much farther do you think it is to the border, Mizella?"

"Can you see the last car in front of us?"

"I can't."

"When you do, we have arrived at the border."

Chapter 27

The Polish-Romanian border is a beehive of activity with refugees trying to cross beyond a German checkpoint. Lieutenant Henningsen is pacing back and forth in front of his men. He stops in front of his sergeant. "If they leave Poland, they must come through this checkpoint, Sergeant. Be on the constant lookout, check every car, every occupant. Find them. They are three young men, and I've learned they are traveling with a young woman too. They have stolen one of our most valuable assets. Find them. Stop them."

"What if they leave Poland at some other point along the border?"

"I have men stationed along the border, Sergeant. They have no other way to escape."

"Do you want them arrested?"

Henningsen shakes his head with no remorse or conscience. "I want them shot and their bodies hanged from a tree as a warning to anyone else who tries to defy the Fatherland, or us."

"They will not escape through here, sir."

"If they do, God help us all."

Wolfgang leans against the roadster. It's early evening, and the procession of refugees has come to a complete stop.

Patrycja steps from the car. "What's the hold-up?"

"Some car at the head of the line. The Germans won't let the old man drive into Romania, and he's causing quite a stir." They turn their heads at the sound of a shot.

"My God, they've killed him, Wolfgang. What will they do to us?"

"Nothing. Our papers are in order. We are Polish citizens seeking asylum in Romania. Just smile and be courteous. Let them see your legs. Wink if you have to. We'll make it through okay."

"What if they find Baby?"

"We won't see tomorrow."

"That's encouraging."

"Our mission was a long shot when we started. It's even longer now."

Wolfgang and Patrycja are startled when a gypsy wagon pulls alongside the roadster. Ferdek jumps to the ground ahead of Tavius. Patrycja leaps from the roadster and grabs Ferdek around the neck with one hand while feeling for Tavius with the other.

Patrycja declares, "You're alive! I was so afraid I would never see either of you again. I've been sick to my stomach ever since you left."

Ferdek says, "We've had better days, but this one is turning out all right."

Patrycja uses the side of her hand to wipe the dried blood from his face. Ferdek smiles. "It's not mine."

Wolfgang shakes Mizella's hand. "I never thought we'd see you again."

Mizella grins at Wolfgang. "We made a little trade, the boys and me. They saved my daughter, and I offered to give them a ride to the border. Why not? I was coming here anyway."

Patrycja sees Halina for the first time. She gasps at the blood covering the girl.

Halina smiles. "The blood's not mine either."

Patrycja faces Ferdek and Tavius. "Well, don't keep us in suspense. What did you find in Brest Litovsk?"

"We'll talk about it later, sister."

Ferdek turns to Wolfgang. "Do you have a plan for getting Baby across the border?"

"I wasn't expecting a German checkpoint. It will be dicey."

"Why do you think the Germans are searching every vehicle that passes through here?"

"Standard procedure, I assume."

"You may be right. But I think they're looking for Baby. If they kill us too, that's even better."

Tavius asks, "Do you have a plan, Ferdek?"

Ferdek confirms with a nod and a smile. "I do if Mizella will sell me his wagon."

Mizella eyes open wide in shock. "What will I do without my wagon?"

"I will give you a thousand Polish zlotys, cash in hand."

"I will buy several wagons, Ferdek. That's what I'll do."

"Does it come with the dynamite in the back?"

"For a thousand polish zlotys, it comes with everything but Halina."

Ferdek reaches into the back floorboard of the roadster and retrieves his backpack, handing Mizella the funds.

Ferdek announces, "We've made it this far, and we don't have much farther to go." He holds up the backpack. "Baby is almost home."

The procession of cars finally inches forward, and everyone morphs into character for the next phase.

Chapter 28

It is almost dusk as Wolfgang and Patrycja drive slowly up the checkpoint and stop at the wooden gate separating Poland from Romania. General Eberhardt swaggers over, eyeing the roadster. "A beautiful car."

Wolfgang refuses to look at him, concealing his face.

"It's a shame that I must confiscate such a magnificent machine. But I'm sure you know all about the spoils of war."

Wolfgang opens his mouth to argue when a German sergeant rips open the door and drags Wolfgang out of the car by the shoulder, throwing him on the ground. The soldier shoves the barrel of his rifle against Wolfgang's throat.

Patrycja exits the roadster, steps over Wolfgang, and walks seductively to the general. She smiles and winks. "I come with the car."

Eberhardt looks down at Wolfgang as he asks, "Your husband?"

"Just a driver."

Patrycja pulls a key from her pocket and waves it in front of the general's face. "Hotel Czernowitz, room 242. I do hope you know where it is." She coyly scratches the key across the general's chin and drops it in his hand.

Eberhardt eyes the beauty with lust. "I am quite familiar with the hotel."

Patrycja winks, and with a sincere, pleading look, requests, "It's a long way for a lady to walk."

"I'll make sure we have a car to take you to the hotel. I'll be there about eight."

"Do bring some champagne. A lady does love champagne when she's entertaining a gentleman caller for the first time."

Patrycja and the general are interrupted by a commotion and men shouting. A gypsy wagon roars toward the border, the horses galloping as hard as they can go. Ferdek crouches in the wagon, urging the horses faster as soldiers fire. Bullets hammer the side of the wagon.

Lieutenant Henningsen races with his men toward the wagon as it breaks past the checkpoint. "He's the one. Stop him."

The wagon careens sideways as it crosses a ditch, when the horses break free at a gallop. Ferdek falls to the ground. He loses the backpack as he rolls away from the gunfire but is up quickly and sprinting toward the forest.

Henningsen scrambles for the backpack, picks it up, and holds it triumphantly over his head. "Success. We have it in our possession, sir."

At that very moment, the backpack explodes, killing Henningsen with the blast. Wood shards from the wagon fly everywhere, forcing everyone to the ground. By the time the stunned soldiers look up, Ferdek is gone.

Chapter 29

The roadster glides down the street and stops in front of the hotel Czernowitz in Cernauti. General Eberhardt steps out and straightens his jacket. Pleased to arrive on time, he carries the promised bottle of champagne. Grinning, he jogs up the steps and walks eagerly into the hotel.

Ferdek, Tavius, and Wolfgang watch from the shadows, then slip out of the alley and make their way to a parked vehicle. Tavius crawls under the roadster. He works a second backpack free from its hiding place, then he slides out with the all-important cargo.

Grinning, Tavius compliments his friend. "Ingenious, Ferdek."

"I didn't think we had a chance to smuggle Baby to Romania, but no one would stop a general and search his car."

Wolfgang asks, "How did you know the general would confiscate the car?"

"Simple. He's a German general."

Inside the Czernowitz, General Eberhardt goes to the second floor, confidently striding down the hallway. He ceremoniously pulls the key from his pocket and kisses it in anticipation. The general steps in front of room 242 and tries the key in the lock, but it doesn't turn. He tries again with the same results. Agitated, he knocks on the door.

Outside the hotel, Tavius works quickly to hotwire the roadster. After a few anxious moments, he steps to one side. "Hit it." The engine roars to life.

Tavius and Ferdek jump into the back seat with Wolfgang driving. He stops in front of the alley. Patrycja runs to the roadster and climbs into the front seat. They zip out of town.

Upstairs in the hotel, a frustrated General Eberhardt is still knocking on the door. His knocking become more frantic with each passing moment. Finally, he smashes the bottle of champagne against the door and storms back down the hallway.

Chapter 30

After days of driving and dodging retreating troops, Ferdek, Tavius, Wolfgang, and Patrycja arrive at the British Embassy. Parking the roadster, they get out and walk to the front door. They are worn and disheveled, their clothes rumpled, the men badly in need of a shower and shave. Ferdek and Tavius still wear bloodstains on their faces.

Ferdek, carrying a suitcase, pushes the buzzer. Everyone waits.

The embassy door opens. An attaché wearing a suit, starched white shirt, and black tie stands in the doorway. The man shifts his gaze between the faces of the visitors.

Ferdek announces, "We are here to see your ambassador."

The man rolls his eyes in disgust and blandly replies, "He is not accepting appointments this morning."

Tavius says, "We don't have an appointment."

With that, the attaché starts to close the door. "The ambassador is not accepting guests this morning either."

Wolfgang places his hand firmly against the door, then blocks it with his booted foot.

"Here is our letter of introduction." Ferdek pulls a well-worn, dirt-stained envelope from his back pocket and hands it to the attaché.

The attaché scans the letter and steps back to allow them entrance. "The ambassador will see you momentarily."

After delivering the letter of introduction to the British ambassador they only have to wait a few moments before the attaché returns to escort them into his office.

The ambassador is sitting at his desk, rereading the letter as the attaché announces them. Ferdek, Tavius, Wolfgang, and Patrycja enter the inner sanctum as the man takes a look at his visitors.

The British ambassador has a stiff upper lip. "This is all highly unusual."

Ferdek agrees, "Indeed it is, sir."

"The Polish ambassador requests that I meet with you immediately, and I don't even know who you are."

Tavius steps forward. "It doesn't matter who we are. What matters is what we've done."

Ferdek places the suitcase on the desk and opens it. He carefully removes a machine and sets it in front of the man. "Compliments of Ambassador Ferdek Watcowski."

The British Ambassador stands and stares down at the machine. His ordinarily stoic features are quickly replaced with confusion and uncertainty. "What is this?"

Wolfgang proudly states, "That, Mr. Ambassador, is a German enigma machine."

Tavius explains, "Your government and the allied forces have wanted one for a long time. Your wait is over."

"The enigma machine encodes then decodes all German messages." Ferdek adds, "Your army will be able to know the secrets, plans, strategies, and movements of the German forces as soon as the Germans plan them."

"My God, man, this machine will change the war."

Patrycja smiles, thrilled to be a part of the delivery of the machine. "Your military leaders won't be in the dark anymore."

"Our role was to get it here, sir," Ferdek explains. "We are confident you will make sure it reaches the right hands."

"Of course, but where did you get it?"

Tavius sighs and looks weary. "That, sir, is a rather long and complicated story.

"Do the Germans know you have it?"

Ferdek says, "The Germans believe it was destroyed in a bomb blast. It's our little secret now."

The ambassador stares hard at each face. "Who are you? This enigma machine is so vital to our effort, I need to know who we owe so much to."

Patrycja winks and grins. "Just consider us Procurement and Delivery."

A four of them turn without another word and stride toward the door, leaving the ambassador with a puzzled look on his face.

Once outside the British embassy, the team of Patrycja, Ferdek, Tavius, and Wolfgang walk up to the roadster and stop to eye one another. They are tired but satisfied in completing their mission, but their minds are racing.

"I trust you still have it, Ferdek," Wolfgang asks.

Ferdek smiles and pats his breast pocket. "We've got the blueprints. We can build machines of our own. We can stop Nazis and evil everywhere. All I need now is a good blacksmith."

Wolfgang broadly smiles. "I just happen to know of a competent blacksmith who lives close to my family's chalet."

Tavius arches his brow. "Has he been known to build the most delicate of metal castings? Say like a series of precision rotors?"

Wolfgang nods and smiles. "Gentlemen and lady, I would maintain that we too should learn the secrets of the enigma machine so we can put a stop to the Nazis. We owe it to Poland."

Patrycja aggressively folds her arms in front of her chest. With a stern look, she demands, "Why can't this weapon be used to penetrate any evil aggressor? Doesn't evil always plan, believing no one can read their communications?"

Tavius brightens at the new twist. "What about the good people and governments that need their information protected? Why can't we learn to do both?"

Wolfgang and Ferdek both nod and smile. Wolfgang adds, "Why not indeed."

About the Authors

Breakfield – Works for a high-tech manufacturer as a solution architect, functioning in hybrid data/telecom environments. He considers himself a long-time technology geek, who also enjoys writing, studying World War II history, travel, and cultural exchanges. Charles' love of wine tastings, cooking, and Harley riding has found ways into the stories. As a child, he moved often because of his father's military career, which even helps him withthe various character perspectives he helps bring to life in the series. He continues to try to teach Burkey humor.

Burkey – Works as a business architect who builds solutions for customers on a good technology foundation. She has written many technology papers, white papers, but finds the freedom of writing fiction a lot more fun. As a child, she helped to lead the kids with exciting new adventures built on make believe characters, was a Girl Scout until high school, and contributed to the community as a young member of a Head Start program. Rox enjoys family, learning, listening to people, travel, outdoor activities, sewing, cooking, and thinking about how to diversify the series.

Breakfield and Burkey – started writing non-fictional papers and books, but it wasn't nearly as fun as writing fictional stories. They found it interesting to use the aspects of technology that people are incorporating into their daily lives more and more as a perfect way to create a good guy/bad guy story with elements of travel to the various places they have visited either professionally and personally, humor, romance, intrigue, suspense, and a spirited way to remember people who have crossed paths with them. They love to talk about their stories with private and public book readings. Burkey also conducts regular interviews for Texas authors, which she finds very interesting. Her first interview was, wait for it, Breakfield. You can often find them at local book fairs or other family-oriented events.

The primary series is based on a family organization called R-Group. Recently they have spawned a subgroup that contains some of the original characters as the Cyber Assassins Technology Services (CATS) team. The authors have ideas for continuing the series in both of these tracks. They track their diverse characters on a spreadsheet, with a hidden avenue for the future coined The Enigma Chronicles tagged in some portions of the stories. Fan reviews seem to frequently suggest that these would make good television or movie stories, so the possibilities appear endless, just like their ideas for new stories.

They have book video trailers for each of the stories, which can be viewed on YouTube, Amazon's Authors page, or on their website, *www.EnigmaBookSeries.com*. Their website is routinely updated with new interviews, answers to readers' questions, book trailers, and contests. You may also find it fascinating to check out the fun acronyms they create for the stories summarized on their website. Reach out to them at *Authors@EnigmaSeries.com*, *Twitter@EnigmaSeries*, or *Facebook @TheEnigmaSeries*.

> *We would greatly appreciate*
> *if you would take a few minutes*
> *and provide a review of this work on*
> *Amazon, Goodreads and*
> *any of your other favorite places.*
> *We appreciate the feedback.*

Stories by Breakfield and Burkey in The Enigma Series are at www.EnigmaBookSeries.com

A 21st Century Techno Thriller Series
Book Seven
THE ENIGMA GAMERS
A CATS TALE
BREAKFIELD AND BURKEY
The Enigma Dragon
A CATS Tale
A 21st Century Techno Thriller Series
Book Eight
THE ENIGMA BROKER
BREAKFIELD AND BURKEY
the Enigma Threat
eakfield and Burkey
Book 10 From The Enigma Series
THE ENIGMA SOURCE
Breakfield and Bu
the Enigma Beyond
Who Won the AI Wars
BOOK 11: Award Winning Techno-Thriller Series
Breakfield and Burkey

Short Stories by Breakfield and Burkey available on Amazon